D1435287

ALSO BY JULIA OLIVER

Seventeen Times as High as the Moon

Goodbye to the Buttermilk Sky

Music of Falling Water

Devotion

Devotion

A novel based on the life of Winnie Davis,
Daughter of the Confederacy

JULIA OLIVER

The University of Georgia Press   *Athens & London*

Published by the University of Georgia Press

Athens, Georgia 30602

Copyright © 2006 by Julia Oliver

Designed by Erin Kirk New

Set in New Baskerville

Printed and bound by Thomson-Shore

Frontispiece: Portrait of Varina Anne (Winnie) Davis
by A. G. Heaton, 1892. Reproduced by permission of
Confederate Memorial Hall, New Orleans, La.
Photographed by Claude Levet.

The paper in this book meets the guidelines for
permanence and durability of the Committee on
Production Guidelines for Book Longevity of the
Council on Library Resources.

Printed in the United States of America

10   09   08   07   06   C   5   4   3   2   1

Library of Congress Cataloging-in-Publication Data

Oliver, Julia.
Devotion : a novel / Julia Oliver.
    p.   cm.
ISBN-13: 978-0-8203-2874-4 (hardcover : alk. paper)
ISBN-10: 0-8203-2874-X (hardcover : alk. paper)
1. Davis, Varina Anne, 1864–1898—Fiction.
2. United States—History—Civil War, 1861–1865—Fiction.
3. Children of presidents—Confederate States of America—Fiction.
4. Confederate States of America—Fiction. I. Title.
PS3565.L477D48 2006
813'.54—dc22   2006014102

British Library Cataloging-in-Publication Data available

For My Family

I only know that none ever measured

the height and breadth and depth of the soul

of Winnie Davis. It brought a secret into the world;

it carried it out. No one ever guessed it.

—HARRY STILLWELL EDWARDS, 1899

Winnie's Notebook

JULY 25, 1898

In the dream, the junction could be a mural or a mirage. The sky is an improbable larkspur blue; the station house resembles a cuckoo clock that I had as a child and believed was haunted. Bystanders appear inanimate until a turbaned woman the color of a fine piano glides toward me with a basket of peaches. Murmuring in the rich timbre of her race, she places a piece of her fruit in my hand; I feel as though I have received a blessing. Now she's some distance away, standing guard over a long wooden box, and I am lying on the ground with my eyes sealed shut. Above me, in the patois of the deeply rural South, a dialogue commences:

"Lord a mercy, poor thing just folded like a fan."

"She's no poor thing. This is Winnie Davis, the Daughter of the Confederacy. She's also the daughter of the man who was responsible for our troubles."

"Shouldn't heap all the blame on Jefferson Davis. Some say if not for him, we'd have lost the War sooner than we did—"

"—in which case there would have been less bloodshed and poverty. Looks like she's still breathing. Maybe a little slap will bring her around—"

The slap opens my eyes and gets me to a sitting position. I am relieved to find the scratchy bombazine skirt has not risen higher than my ankles.

The conductor asks these two, whose dough-colored faces are almost hidden by sunbonnet brims, to escort me back to the car. The more contentious one asks which side I'm on. "There are no sides to a circle," I say as I give each of them a small pasteboard rectangle imprinted with my name and "The Daughter of the Confederacy" beneath my half-faced likeness. They stare suspiciously at the photographs, as though I am trying to deceive them. . . . They're left behind, but their magpie thoughts follow me onto the train: *The South lays claim to Winnie Davis, yet she has chosen to live in the North. . . . People bow and scrape to her, but her face is overrun with sadness. . . . She ought to thank her lucky stars she doesn't have to hoe and plow.*

The rocky red terrain gives way to a grass-covered slope beside a glistening river. At the forefront of a group of mourners, my swooning mother, draped in black chiffon like the mirrors in a house of death, is flanked by Maggie and Kate, both in severe but stylish mourning garb. Fred stands apart from everyone else. As a breeze becomes my hand and ruffles his hair, he looks as though he sees an apparition. Now they are in the past, and I am being hurtled alone, to God knows where. . . .

The tall, thin conductor stoops to admonish me in a stern, stentorian voice: "Miss Davis, you've a long way to go, and we're not out of Georgia yet. I can't be watching every time we pause at a whistle-stop to make sure you're not left behind."

I give him my word I will not get off again until we arrive at my destination. Or maybe I say "my destiny." When next I see the man, I am fully conscious, and he is shorter, more solid, and less formidable than his Doppelgänger. The train shakes as though it will fly apart at any second, but it is reassuring to know we are on the right track, headed North (in the South, the East is called the North), and moving along at a steady clip.

I have almost drifted off again when he coughs to get my attention. "Ma'am, I noticed you declined to go to the dining car earlier, yet you devoured a peach back there as though your life depended on it. Are you feeling better now?"

"Yes. Thank you for your concern." I'm aware of a film of dried nectar on my mouth and chin. "I can't recall whether I paid for that peach. Did you happen to notice—?"

"I heard the woman say it was a gift. She also said the time has come for you to forgive anybody you need to, including yourself." His forehead creases with the burden of wondering why he felt obliged to relay a message gleaned from eavesdropping on someone else's dream. As he plods on along the narrow, quivering aisle, shaking his head as though to wake himself, I find crumpled in my fist a packet that had contained a hundred cartes de visite of my face in profile. Two were left when the convention ended; now there are none.

It has been my experience that premonition loses its force when the imagery fades. But in this instance, where the content of a dream has merged with reality, the portent is as clear as a mountain spring: On my next journey, I won't be traveling upright.

JULY 27

In the ivory glow of morning, the room's impersonality is gentled by familiar details—Varina's spectacles marking her place in an open book, a vase of feathers from Jeff's peafowl, and on an étagère across from this bed, two winged paperweights that stand apart from furnished bric-a-brac and each other: a Confederate eagle, one of the emblems of four years that have branded my family for going on four decades; the alabaster angel, a souvenir of love I fell into with no thought of consequence. The defining elements are intact, but the last three days have sizeable gaps.

The spell came on in Atlanta with a flash of yellow like spilled paint before my eyes and a jabbing pain behind them. I had just been assigned to a vehicle for the Peachtree Street Parade, and I didn't have with me the flacon of diluted arsenic my mother had provided for throbbing headache. In the congestion of queued-up buggies and brigades, returning to the hotel was not an option, so I tried to forestall the pain with mental effort, which was working to some extent. Then in what seemed divine rebuke for putting my own will on a level with the Almighty's, an unexpected shower descended on the open carriage. Although I arrived at Exposition Hall in garments that clung like seaweed, my black silk jacket and skirt were nearly dry—the auditorium was hot enough to cook a turkey—by the time an honor guard escorted me to the stage where local beauties in white dresses, each banded by a sash imprinted with the name of a military camp or division, were arrayed like scenery. On both sides of the aisle, men in butternut-dyed garments that reeked of battlefields and musty trunks murmured as I passed—*Yessir, that's Jeff's girl all right, she looks just like him; I saw them together at the New Orleans reunion, must have been close to ten years ago. . . . Bless you, Miss Winnie, we loved your papa, God rest his soul.* As I approached the podium, applause swelled to a drum-like roll, the girls' demeanors shifted from demure awareness of their celebrity—their pictures had been on display for a month in the *Confederate Veterans' Magazine*—to bold come-hitherness, and a wave of euphoria such as lovers experience spread through the assembly. That phenomenon of inexplicable, heart-pounding rapture always occurs as some point during these gatherings, and sometimes more than once.

At first, men who had not lost their confidence when they lost the War (or even in its punitive aftermath) and who still went by General or Colonel or Major although their fighting force had long been dissolved, would introduce me, then speak for me. The phrases varied, but the message was always proudly defiant: *Our chieftain's daughter would have you know there is no dishonor in having fought for the South's great cause. She urges you to take heart, and take pride in your heritage. Never apologize for having defended your homes and principles against the Northern aggressors. . . .*

When I began to compose and deliver my own discourses, they took on a more conciliatory manner: *Once again, a grateful South salutes you, its stoic heroes; your sacrifices will not be forgotten as our reunited nation continues to heal and becomes stronger with each passing year. . . .* Not that much of it sinks in. What they really come for is the camaraderie—the whiskey drinking, reminiscing, and renewing of old bonds.

I had finished my address to the United Confederate Veterans' Reunion in Atlanta and braced for a barrage of cane-and-crutch tapping when I felt a bloom of fever rash begin to creep over my flesh like a poison vine. One of the efficient women in charge fetched me a cup of lemonade and a folded, camphor-soaked handkerchief to sniff. It was obvious, by the proud tilt of her head and the way she wore her years, that she numbered herself among the empowered females who, when their sweethearts, husbands, sons, brothers, and fathers went off to the War, stepped up and filled the gap. They ran the plantations and farms; kept the books better than the men had; fended off marauders and rapists; tended children, livestock, wounded soldiers, and the elderly. Some of them stood up all day at desks, cutting sheets of newly printed Confederate notes apart. In recent years—since Reconstruction ended and the insurgents packed up their carpetbags and went back to where they came from—the women have banded together to raise money to build monuments to the Confederate dead and beautify the cemeteries where they are buried. They also help put on these lavish, large-scale gatherings that perpetuate the memory of the South's gallant stand without casting aspersion on the Republic. In the decorated halls where the events are held, the national Stars and Stripes is companionably displayed with the battle flag of the Confederacy—the former as a symbol of the reunited nation, the latter as a memorial. As the *Richmond Examiner* editor Edward Pollard observed in *The Lost Cause*, which he published the year after the War ended, the South acknowledges the restoration of the Union and the ending of slavery, but the epic conflict "did not decide the right of a people to show dignity in misfortune, and to maintain self-respect in the face of adversity. And these are things the Southern people will cling to, still claim, and still assert in their rights and views."

The public part of the celebration ended on Saturday in sunshine bright as a new coin, with a brass band playing the rallying song as hundreds, maybe thousands—they were clumped like birds on sidewalks, patches of ground, the lower limbs of trees, and balconies—clapped and sang with exuberance. The enigmatic phrase "Look-away, Dixie Land" was still reverberating in my head two hours later, as I dressed for the Grand Ball.

Invigorated by a bath and two packets of pharmaceutical headache remedy (I never found the arsenic), I covered the rash on my face and neck with perle powder and buttoned myself into a near-weightless gown of ivory chiffon, a hand-me-down from Kate that exuded her unique essence of generosity, extravagance, and Parisian perfume. Then came blankness darker than the night it obliterated. I awoke to the cacophony of a city in early morning: the cymbalic clang of trolley bells, the amorous murmur of doves on a window ledge, and the singsong hawking of newspaper boys on a steaming sidewalk three floors below. My undergarments were puddled on the carpet, although I was still more or less encased in Kate's frock, which had a transparent ruby-colored stain on its ruched bodice. Apparently, I had attended the gala in the Kimball House ballroom long enough to spill the contents of a wine glass, but I have no recollection of that festivity or of returning to my room in the same hotel, and little of the journey back to Rhode Island until it ended with a squealing halt at the gaslit terminal where Varina (my mother, companion, colleague) and Mr. Burns, proprietor of our summer lodgings, awaited me. Viewed through a soot-streaked window, Varina's moonlike face reflected an even blend of optimism and anxiety. I could imagine the telegraph she'd received: *Miss Davis was taken ill yesterday, and despite our urging that she postpone her return, has insisted on departing as scheduled.*

As a physician summoned by Mr. Burns examined me with his eyes half-closed, I kept mine open, so I would not be tempted to imagine his hands were someone else's. He pronounced my heart and lungs strong, then deferred to my mother's practical diagnosis: "Winnie inherited a susceptibility to slow fevers from her father. She won't require special nursing, and can recuperate here." Here being this compact suite in the Rockingham Hotel at Narragansett Pier, where palatial summer residences rival those of Newport, across the bay.

Varina has spent the night, what part of it she wasn't ministering to me, on a cot she had brought in. At the sound of a cough I could not hold back, she jerks to consciousness, shifts her bulk to the edge of this mattress, touches my forehead with the back of her hand, and says briskly, "You're definitely better. Not as flushed, and cooler." Then in her melodic company voice, as though there are others besides me to hear, "Darling, I wish I could take you home to convalesce."

The word *home* pines like a distant cowbell. "Where would that be?"

"Where indeed." My mother sighs and shakes her head, as though the notion that I might be bound by sentiment to a piece of geography, as most people are, is ridiculous. For her, there would be choices: Home could bring to mind the valentine house of her childhood on a river bluff near Natchez, or the cotton plantation near Vicksburg where she spent the honeyed early years of her marriage, or the stately, borrowed mansion in Richmond, where for four tempestuous years she was chatelaine for a renegade nation.

Varina's owlish eyes, which for a moment seemed to reflect my thoughts, rove restlessly from windows to the door as she comes up with an excuse to leave the sickroom. "It's not yet eight o'clock. Lie still and rest while I see about breakfast."

As though I could be still and rest without thinking or dreaming.

In addition to the borrowed mansion (where I was born, and which we left before my first birthday), I have lived in a military fortress, a foreign academy, boarding and rental houses, the residences of friends and sympathetic strangers, hotels (as a young child, I had the run of the Peabody in Memphis; currently, our main address is the Gerard, in New York), and a somewhat ramshackle, seaside house near Biloxi, Mississippi. From my perspective, the last named would be the logical answer to the question my mother has sidestepped. But not from hers.

Varina Howell Davis's antagonism toward Beauvoir began before she ever saw it. Twelve years after the North defeated the South in the War Between the States, her husband Jefferson Davis returned from a trip to Europe convinced the latest business venture with which he had become associated—an ambitious scheme to promote international trade via the Port of New Orleans—was not likely to succeed. Then almost seventy, Jeff had decided to give up on the world of commerce and look for a tranquil place where he could write his manifesto about the War. The search bore fruit almost immediately: A longtime friend invited him to take up residence at her secluded estate on the Mississippi Gulf Coast. I can imagine that proud man's relief as he inclined his head in gratitude that contained no hint of humility.

My mother, who was still abroad, learned of this development in a newspaper article. She had asked her husband not to settle in that mosquito-plagued region; however, she was used to having her wishes ignored when they didn't coincide with his. What bothered her most was how the public would regard the arrangement. Long aware of Jeff's penchant for forming close bonds with women in their political, social, and family circles, V. had tried to regard such attachments as harmless diversion for a heavily burdened man—but the widow who had issued that invitation was a force to be reckoned with. Except for the fact that she was wealthy and my mother was not, the two women had much in common. Both had been reared in the exclusive cotton-capital society of the lower Mississippi River region. At the age of forty-eight (Varina was then fifty-one), vivacious though not a beauty (as V. was often described), possessed of a brilliant, cultivated mind (attributes Varina also was known for), Sarah Ellis Dorsey appropriated the former President of the Confederate States of America with that offer of haven in a setting he would come to regard as being as near to Paradise as one could find on earth. Jeff thought, or would claim to have thought, that his wife would be thrilled over the opportunity to renew a friendship she had enjoyed as a girl.

He assured her everything was within the realm of propriety. He was a paying guest and did not live in the main house; their oldest son, twenty-year-old Jeff Davis Jr., was a frequent visitor; Mrs. Dorsey's companion cousin, a Mrs. Cochran, and Major Walthall, who was assisting with my father's literary project, were also on the premises. But Varina adamantly refused to join the ménage. She continued to visit her recently married sister in Liverpool and other expatriates from the American South who had migrated to England and France. Briefly, until her presence became a problem, my mother occupied a guest room at the austere institution in Germany where I was then a student. When she'd worn out her welcomes on that side of the ocean, she made her way to Memphis and the home of my sister Maggie and Maggie's kind, genial husband, Addison Hayes. Jeff had been at Beauvoir for almost two years when Varina haughtily accepted Sarah Dorsey's long-standing invitation, not because she feared she might lose her husband—Maggie says she never acknowledged that possibility—but because she had nowhere else to go. By the time I came to live there, Mrs. Dorsey had died of cancer and bequeathed the property to my father, and my mother was very much in residence.

I had studied photographs and memorized the description in Jeff's letters, but seeing Beauvoir for the first time was an epiphany. I assumed the simultaneous feeling of relief and a sense of having been there before was a universal reaction to homecoming. The sentiment was also rooted in Jeff's instructions to Maggie, Jeff Jr., and me to think of Mississippi as our native land, although none of his and Varina's six children except the first, Samuel, who died in his second year, had been born there.

Surrounded by cedar, magnolia, and moss-infested live oak trees, the main house projected hospitality like a confident hostess's smile. The single-story, raised-cottage design was practical and aesthetically appealing: Tall, down-to-the-floor windows and high ceilings encouraged ventilation; understated elements of Greek Revival architecture provided an aura of refinement without ostentation. Jeff had turned the cottage he originally inhabited—one of a pair of enclosed pavilions with pagoda-style roofs—into an office and library. The other was for guests, among whom were circuit-riding preachers of the Methodist Church. (My parents attended an Episcopal chapel, where I would soon be pressed into service as organist, but Varina is more gregarious than religious, and on the sleepy Gulf Coast in the early 1880s, Methodist tent revivals were popular social events.) Beyond the building complex, several acres of scuppernong vineyards and a grove of orange trees provided a misleading ambience of prosperity and industry.

V. had taken as her special project a circular rose garden, divided with crosswalks and surrounded by fruit trees, which extended from the dogtrot kitchen and servants' quarters to Oyster Bayou, a freshwater stream that crosses the wooded back portion of the property. During my first weeks at Beauvoir, I had nightly forebodings that these reassuring trappings of domesticity would disappear while I slept. My sister, who is nine years older than I, had told me how servants at the Executive Mansion in Richmond began to leave during the last months of the War. Some slipped away in the night, without saying good-bye. Each time she realized she would never see a familiar dark face again, Maggie wept as hard as she had at little brother Joe's funeral the year before. "God gave you to us, in Joe's place," she said. "Not that I had prayed for a baby sister."

When I was half a world away at school, a letter from my father would elicit an olfactory memory of cigars, pipe tobacco, cloves, liniment, and toilet soap. As he embraced me for the first time after that long separation, I realized this hodgepodge of scents was a disparate combination of rugged masculinity and near-dandified fastidiousness. He was not as robust as I recalled or imagined, and I'd forgotten his left eye was shrouded with a cloud of white, as though it had died before the rest of him. In addition to partial blindness, facial neuralgia, and occasional bronchial problems, he contended with rheumatism, which his wife blamed on a wound he'd received thirty-four years before, in the Mexican War he had promised her he would not go to. Jeff attributed his infirmities to God's will and did not complain.

I called him Father while he was alive. Now I find it easier to think of him with the nickname he was known by to most people, whether friend or foe. These references to my mother with her first name and its initial, which are also mine, are not meant as disrespectful; she took to signing herself "V. Jefferson-Davis" almost nine years ago, after her husband died.

When I was eleven, Jeff decided I would attend a Protestant boarding school in Germany. He had overruled Varina's suggestion of Paris, where Maggie had attended a school run by nuns, as he had come to believe that city was utterly lascivious, therefore inappropriate for a young girl whose parents would be on another continent. The Friedlander Institute in Karlsruhe was at the edge of a royal park surrounding the Baroque palace built by Margrave Karl Wilhelm, the city's founder, in the previous century. The starkly beautiful setting reminded me of the scariest fairy tales. Over much of the ground, a carpet of moss in a garish shade of green—like the eyeshades worn by railway agents—reflected the sparse sunlight that trickled through dense stands of fir and pine. For weeks after I arrived, I slept with my large leather Bible and pretended it was my mother's warm flesh.

Five years later, when my parents came to Europe to retrieve me, my father was surprised to see I was almost as tall as Varina, who stood within an inch of the top of his head.

"It's fashionable now for young women to be statuesque," she told him. "And fortunately, Winnie takes after you in facial features. Her eyes and mouth are strikingly similar to yours, dearest."

Jeff murmured, "Poor child," and flushed with pleasure. I knew at that instant I would never again be jealous when someone remarked on Maggie's striking resemblance to our dark-haired, dark-eyed mother. I was seventeen, a year younger than Varina had been when she married a widower twice her age. Jeff's eldest brother, Joseph Davis, had brought the two together and encouraged the match. The qualities these men initially found appealing in Varina Howell—her vivacious curiosity, quick wit, and confident free-spiritedness—did not bode well in her new status as the wife of one of them. Like most of the ante-bellum, Southern planter hierarchy, the Davis brothers were authoritarian and paternalistic toward their spouses. Urged on by Joseph, Jeff set out to modify his bride's temperament. The process vacillated from firm persuasion to didactic command and had to be repeated every so often. She would make a genuine effort to be the submissive helpmate her husband required, but what my sister called our mother's cussed streak of independence would not be exorcised altogether. By the time I was five, I no longer flinched when she hurled a plate against a wall or spouted a tirade of rhetoric. I had assumed it was natural for a grown woman to throw a tantrum or speak out on any subject she chose to, until Maggie explained that was not so. Women were supposed to promote decorum, not disrupt it, and most of them did—it was just our mother who was out of step. Even so, Maggie defended her: "She's obliged by her nature to let off steam occasionally, otherwise she might explode."

"What does explode mean?" Before I learned to read, Maggie was my dictionary and encyclopedia.

"Like in the War, when the cannons blasted outside Richmond. The sound carried for miles, and you could see it light up the sky." She added, with a sigh of exaggerated condescension, "Oh, I keep forgetting—you can't remember back then."

After I returned to this country from Germany, I knew very little about the War that was three-fourths over when I was born. As

I began to amass a store of fact and hearsay on the subject, I analyzed it from my own perspective. For instance, my conception in September 1863 had occurred at a time when my father was elated over the Confederate Army of Tennessee's victory in the Battle of Chickamauga. Then the tide turned: As my mother began to wear loose clothing to accommodate the bulge of pregnancy, Union President Abraham Lincoln made headlines around the world with his eloquent address at Gettysburg, and Union General Ulysses S. Grant avenged their loss at Chickamauga with the capture of Chattanooga, Tennessee. Near the time of Varina's confinement, General Grant advanced toward Richmond to take on General Lee's Army of Northern Virginia, and General Sherman fought his way toward the Confederate stronghold of Atlanta. Two weeks before I came into the world on June 27, 1864, the tide turned again, as Union forces bungled a chance to capture Petersburg, Virginia, and cut off the Confederate rail lines. The only person I explained to was Fred: "Those validating circumstances proved I was more than an inconvenient accident."

He replied, in his cheerful, soothing voice, "Try not to see yourself as a product of that tragic era, Winnie. That was their time; this is ours: yours and mine."

By then—it was his second or third visit to Beauvoir—Fred was comfortable with my parents. That night over dinner, during an amiable discussion of the current political climate, he volunteered the information that his late father, a Democrat, had been appointed assistant revenue commissioner for their district of New York by the Republican president Abraham Lincoln. Varina's fork paused in midair for a second and the candles on the table sputtered. My father said equably, "Mr. Lincoln was extremely level-headed and used astute judgment."

When we left Paris on that twelve-day crossing in late November 1881, I was apprehensive about the country to which I was returning. What I recalled most of my first eleven years was a precarious feeling of insecurity, due to the groundlessness of not being settled and the skittish up-and-down moods of my parents. The two of them appeared to be in good spirits on this voyage. One of the conversations I heard through the thin partition that separated their stateroom from mine concerned my marriageability.

"Winnie seems more comfortable speaking German than English," Jeff said. "I doubt young men will find that guttural accent attractive."

"It will cease when there's no one around to converse with her in that language," Varina replied airily. "The main obstacle is the lack of a dowry."

"That lack did not stop me from proposing to you."

"Thank God. Oh my dear, I cannot imagine my life without you in it." The depth of her feeling underscored the dramatic force of those words.

I held my breath, hoping Jeff would respond in kind, but he ignored his wife's declaration of love and stuck to the subject: "My most fervent desire is to be able to provide our last child with a comfortable endowment for her future welfare and happiness."

"Her future welfare and happiness will depend on the match she makes," my mother said. They seemed to be in agreement that my best prospects for marrying well would be in New Orleans, where they had many connections—none of whom,

Varina reminded her husband, had offered Jeff employment after he was released from the Federal prison. My father murmured, his voice so low I could scarcely make out the words, "I hope Winnie will be with us for a good while yet." Varina's reply—"Oh, yes, so do I"—surprised me. It wasn't until after Jeff died that she explained she had not wanted me to follow her own example and marry "too young, and to a man who had given the best of his love to a first wife who would forever be in his heart the age she was when he lost her." She doesn't cotton to the idea of being second-best in anything.

"It's not as though he chose Knox Taylor over you. You were barely born when they married," I reminded her, when the subject came up again recently.

"The fact remains that I did not ever have all his love, as she did."

That's the kind of thing I always give her the last word on.

Maggie and her family were frequent visitors to Beauvoir, but Jeff Jr., the handsome, good-natured big brother who used to carry me piggyback around whatever domain we happened to be occupying, had perished during a malaria epidemic in Memphis during the last year I was in Karlsruhe. I was deprived of the comfort of grieving for him simultaneously with the rest of the family, because I did not learn of the tragedy until several weeks later. When it finally came, the poignant letter from my mother began, "I am sorry, darling, that I cannot hold you as I give you this sad news. . . ." A few paragraphs later, she confided, matter-of-factly, "You may recall how superstitious your brother was. A few days before he became ill, he accidentally broke a looking glass. From that moment on, Jeff Jr. was convinced his fortune would change for the worse—and I found myself worrying that he might be right."

According to Varina, only very special people, such as her husband and their favorite son, have intimations of their own mortality. She was not surprised in the least to hear that President Lincoln had a dream of his assassination. I believe everyone may have that prophetic dream of the end of his or her life, but most are fortunate enough not to recognize the vision for what it is.

Previously, I had been appended to my mother or Maggie. On my return, it seemed natural, ordained even, that I would become the close companion of my father. Jeff and I took daily walks around the grounds of Beauvoir House (Varina had added the "House" for her personal stationery, thereby putting her own imprimatur on the title provided by Sarah Dorsey), accompanied by a procession of dogs—in the lead, his favorites, a Newfoundland and a collie—and a strutty, wing-dragging old peacock. In sturdy, high-back oak rockers Jeff had built in his workshop, we spent late afternoons on the wide porch that wrapped around three sides of the house while I read aloud to him from novels by Sir Walter Scott and he recited, from his prodigious bank of memory, the poetry of Robert Burns and Lord Byron.

On cool days, we rode horses on the beach and through a forest that seethed with such tension I once asked if a battle had been fought there. "Not that I'm aware of," he replied. "You may have picked up on something that took place here long ago. There's an old Indian saying that trees retain what they've witnessed." Whenever he spoke of Indian lore, his eyes, even the clouded one, would brighten. He also told me stories of his boyhood in Woodville, Kentucky, and his schooling at Transylvania Academy and the military academy at West Point. Once, when he seemed particularly mellow, I asked what he would do differently if he had his life to live over again. My father answered as though he'd been waiting for the question: "I would be a cavalry officer, and break squares."

On his first visit, Fred Wilkinson and I explored that secretive wooded area and each other on a mat of pine needles beneath the tall trees that had shed them. We had spread the picnic cloth beside a stream banked with wild azalea, which in full bloom looked like flocks of yellow butterflies. In the hamper the cook provided was a carafe of scuppernong wine. When it was empty, we unfastened garments as though in a contest, hardly daring to breathe lest we break the spell. At the moment when I thought we might rise into the hot, silken air like the jays that had made off with crusts and crumbs from our picnic, the trees around us seemed to close in, as if to keep us grounded there. . . . I like to think the magic of that afternoon is stored in the trunks and branches of those silent, observant sentinels, that it wasn't all destroyed.

It is oddly comforting to know that Fred will outlive me: The dream has promised I can run my fingers through his hair, in passing.

My mother had aged more pronouncedly than my father. An accomplished equestrienne in her youth, Varina had given up riding when her heaviness made her more cautious. She who has never been fearful of crossing the ocean on a ship refused to accompany Jeff and me on boat rides in the calm crannies of the sound or even on strolls along the shore. She would stand in the tree shade and watch our backs as we continued, arm in arm, to the end of the narrow pier. That she was too far away to hear the rhythmic pulsing of water against the pilings afforded me some unaccountable satisfaction.

As a welcoming surprise to Beauvoir, my father had designated as mine a small room adjacent to his office and fitted it out with easel, palette, paint box, a small desk, and bookshelves. The door between our ateliers was seldom closed. When I was immersed in writing or painting, the sound of his chair scraping the floor, or a whiff of his pipe or cigar, would reassure me he was close by.

My mother's presence could stir up all the energy in a room, and at her exodus, a feeling of stability would reassert itself. When my father was away, his personality flowed through the house like a gentle, departed spirit, returned to love again. . . I could feel his approving, affectionate gaze on me whenever we were in the same room, and sometimes when we were not. In the evenings after dinner, at his request, I played Chopin preludes and popular music on the Knabe piano, which had a robust, European tone, although the keys tended to stick because of the humid climate.

Varina, her hands and eyes occupied with needlework, would sing or hum with the music, unless she was in a contrary mood. Once, when Jeff requested I play the ballad "Lilly Dale," she stood abruptly, and let the embroidery hoop slide from her lap to the floor. "I despise that maudlin song," she said, and flounced from the room. My father cleared his throat with consternation, but made no comment. The many thoughtful things his wife did to please him could be negated in an instant when her bad temper manifested.

"Romantic airs are usually maudlin," I said. "What does she have against that one?"

"I have no idea," Jeff said wearily. "She knows it's been one of my favorites since Jennie Clay used to sing it at Washington soirees."

Virginia Clay and her statesman husband, Clement Clay of Alabama, had been among the group of captured Confederates on the steamer that transported Jeff to prison at Fortress Monroe, in Norfolk, Virginia. Varina was aboard also, with her four children plus Jim, the mulatto orphan she had taken in some months before. Jeff had made application in the city courts to adopt the boy. Varina explained the situation to a Union Army captain who took the howling child away with him when he left the ship. Maggie heard the Yankee say, "That colored boy will have a better home up North than he would with any Rebs, especially now that most all their houses have been burned." The soldiers snipped buttons off my baby smocks as souvenirs for their wives and cruelly teased Jeff Jr. and Willie; the boys hated it when their captors taunted them by singing "We'll Hang Jeff Davis from a Sour Apple Tree."

Unencumbered with children, Mrs. Clay felt free to speak contemptuously to the guards, and got by with it. "Just imagine how that must have chafed our mother," Maggie said, and I certainly could. I believe I knew then that my sister needed to talk about those times, to get it out of her system. She would relate these happenings to me as though she were full-grown instead of fourteen years old, and I tried to stretch my five years into the comprehension level of at least ten, so she would continue to use me as her sounding board.

Jeff sighed as if he'd been privy to that recollection. After a moment, he said, "Jennie Clay was beautiful, talented, and greatly admired. She still is."

"Is she the lady in the ambrotype portrait on your desk?" It wasn't really a question. According to Maggie, Father was sweet on Mrs. Clay when they were all living in Richmond, and perhaps before that, in Washington. I had come across a quip attributed to a famous Mississippian: "The wives of Clay and Davis, on opposite sides of the parlor, were like two men-of-war firing at each other."

Jeff said, "She gave me the picture when I was at Fortress Monroe. Gazing at that image helped me keep my sanity then. I shall forever cherish Mrs. Clay's thoughtfulness and my recollections of pleasurable hours spent in her company."

That was the only time in my presence he made any reference to his incarceration. The rush of sympathy it elicited was offset by appall that he would attribute any part of his survival of that ordeal to a woman other than his wife. I closed the sheet music and pulled the lid over the keyboard.

He was surprised. "Aren't we going to have our song?"

"Not tonight. I'm tired." I placed my mother's sampler, its inked aphorism more than half worked in precise cross-stitches, on the seat of the Victorian lady's chair she had vacated. Then I left the room without bending over the gentleman's chair to press my lips to his forehead or feel the pressure of his graceful hands on my back or hear him whisper, "Sweet dreams, my angel"—and willed myself not to will him to follow me.

More sensory recall of the last evening in Atlanta: whiffs of pomaded hair, masculine perspiration, and pepperminted breath as a firm hand propels me away from the lights and the music and along a shadowy corridor; a softly drawled avowal to renew "our special friendship" next summer, at the Charleston convention. . . . Then the curtain rings down again. V. has taken a trio of amber glass bottles from my vanity case, held them to the window light, and noted with obvious satisfaction that all are empty. As usual, she sent me off with an arsenal of homeopathic remedies, patent medicines, and her own concoctions. I usually pour the contents out and bring the empty bottles back with me, or leave the bottles unopened on a hotel dresser, in which case she complains that glass does not grow on trees. Since I don't recall emptying or abandoning this latest group, perhaps I imbibed all the contents. Before the ball, or after?

I have made my way on wobbly legs to the bathroom. Jeff's shaving mug is on a shelf above the lavatory, where Varina placed it on the luminously pastel day in early June when we arrived here. A yellow chamois riding glove, still slightly puffed from the imprint of his right hand, accompanied me to and from Atlanta. In such bits and pieces, we keep him with us.

After I returned to this country, I continued to pursue musical disciplines and paint, but my ambition had crystallized into a single focus: I would be a writer. I counted on Beauvoir to nurture that calling in me as it had in my parents and before them, in our benefactress, Mrs. Dorsey. Her novels had been published under a pseudonym, "Filia," which V. said sounded like the name of a frisky mare. Had we known each other, Sarah Dorsey might have become my literary mentor, which would have given my mother another reason to dislike her.

V. would interject here that she herself has done well by me in that role. She provided the supposedly true story on which my novel *The Veiled Doctor* was based and suggested that I make the next one's setting less provincial, with the heroine more like me. I took the first part of that advice, but not the second.

Early last week, she read a brief newspaper item about my forthcoming book aloud to me at breakfast: "Miss Varina Anne Davis, also known as Winnie Davis, has penned a new novel, which according to Harper & Brothers Publishers will be available soon in bookstores and libraries. *A Romance of Summer Seas* takes place on a ship in the China Seas. The unusual love story unfolds in sophisticated prose, through the very credible voice of a wise, observant gentleman."

My mother tossed the paper aside. "I hope the real reviews will be as kind. But someone's bound to point out that it was a risky choice for a female writing under her own name to compose romantic fiction from a male perspective." Normally, she would applaud me for making a risky choice, as long as it didn't have to do with marriage. She was miffed because I had declined to discuss the work with her while it was in progress and had not let her read the manuscript before it was typeset.

I picked up the newspaper and scanned the article. "I wish the piece had included some mention of the two principals."

V. pounced as though the remark were a ball of yarn and she a cat. "Frankly, dear, I didn't find either of that pair as interesting as your observant gentleman narrator. I appreciate your high-mindedness in not modeling characters on people you know, but you should reconsider that premise. Your former fiancé would be the ideal paradigm for a miscast lover."

"I think we've done him enough damage."

"'We'?"

"Actually, you. But since I allowed it, he has good cause to despise both of us." It is difficult for me to speak of Fred Wilkinson. His name rolls around the perimeter of my heart but not off my tongue.

"Your father would never allow such rudeness."

"Not from me, perhaps, but he tolerated much worse from you."

She began to sob in great heaves, as though she might come apart like an overstuffed pillow from its seams.

After she'd quieted down, I said, "Send a wire to Maggie. Tell her I'm too difficult to live with, and ask her to come and rescue you. Maybe you'll be in Colorado by the time I return from the convention."

"Please let's not have this unpleasantness," she whispered. Her face was as gray as her hair.

By way of apology, I fetched my mother the smelling salts and a tin of fudge she thought she had hidden.

Three mostly silent days later, on July 20, I set out for Atlanta. On the train headed South, back to what before my time was the prosperous, slaveholding Land of Cotton, I felt the distance widen anew between my former love and me. Watching the countryside slide by, I saw Fred's reproachful face in the clouds over Virginia and the Carolinas. . . . Now, in my fevered state, I am recalling the only time he ever saw me in the throes of a real spell. He had tried to understand, and he did not give up on me—until we forced him to.

Another elusive piece of the weekend has risen to the surface. In Atlanta, as often happens at these commemorations, I was aware of an undercurrent of animosity toward my mother from those who have never forgiven her for moving us, after Jeff's death, from Mississippi to New York. At the time, the protest had ranged from strong disapproval to outrage. In reference to a New York paper's report that Mrs. Jefferson Davis had paid a call on Mrs. Ulysses S. Grant, an Alabama journalist ranted, "Our fiery leader must be thrashing in his grave at the idea of his consort's sipping tea with the widow of a man whose face was etched on the bottoms of our chamberpots." Varina likes the limelight and she is aware that publicity, even when it's not flattering, helps to keep her there. What she cannot bear is for Jefferson Davis to be ridiculed, criticized, or lied about in print. After reading that clipping, which arrived anonymously, she smiled and said, "Well, it's unusual for Jeff to be described as fiery, but indeed he could be, when the occasion called for it."

Once he was gone, the isolation that had appealed to her husband became intolerable to Varina, and she resented his having left Beauvoir to me. I reminded her that Mrs. Dorsey had specified I would have a reversionary interest in her estate, which she left in its entirety to "my most honored and esteemed friend, Jefferson Davis." I had committed to memory the summation sentence of Sarah Dorsey's last will and testament, but knew better than to recite it to my mother: "I do not intend to share in the ingratitude of my country towards the man, who is in my eyes, the highest and noblest in existence."

Jeff was carrying out the wishes of the previous owner, but also, he would have envisioned his bequest as an incentive that might persuade my fiancé to take up residence in Mississippi. Or perhaps my father realized Fred and I would not marry, and hoped

Beauvoir would be my consolation for the loss of a dream, as it had been for him.

Still, Varina's reasons for leaving were valid. Other than an undependable harvest of citrus fruit, Beauvoir had never been an income-producing plantation; the soil was mostly sand and decayed vegetation. It became even lonelier in the off-season, when our neighbors closed their coastal houses and returned to primary residences in New Orleans. Under the guise of seeking advice from close friends, my mother elaborated on what they already knew: We could not afford to keep up that leisurely way of life. Even before Jeff died, our plight was obvious enough that baskets of food were left on the porch.

During a trip to New York to confer with publishers about her biography of her late husband, Varina accepted an offer of employment from Joseph Pulitzer for the two of us to be special writers for his newspaper. The annual salaries of $1,500 each would enable us to live moderately well in an apartment hotel in that city and pay a caretaker for Beauvoir until such time as an acceptable buyer—one who would not desecrate the property—could be found. Varina told friends and cousins we were moving because, as they were well aware, her health was undermined by the South's oppressive climate. They also knew that nothing keeps her down for long; she has remarkable recuperative powers.

I hope to purchase a cottage at Bar Harbor if the new novel does well, but a more practical goal would be to buy a carriage, so Varina will not have to hire hacks to take her to the theatre. In a panic over money after Jeff died, she sold the large vehicle at Beauvoir for forty dollars. Then she referred dismissively to our only remaining conveyance as "that rickety, backless buggy." In her younger years, V. had a fondness for whatever provided efficient transportation: fine saddle horses, ocean-crossing ships, river-plying steamers, fast passenger trains, sturdy carriages with a well-matched pair of horses. Soon after her husband was elected to head the Southern Secession, she placed an order with a New Orleans firm for an elegant phaeton with silver fittings. It had not been delivered when the new government was moved from Montgomery, Alabama, to Richmond, Virginia. Jeff and his staff left for the new post immediately; Varina stayed in Montgomery to pack up their belongings. At the end of a four-day journey, she, the children, and her sister Margaret Howell were met at the depot by Jeff and an impressive equipage, provided by the city of Richmond, for the first family of the Confederacy to ride in style to their temporary living quarters in the Spotswood Hotel. The interior of that carriage was upholstered in yellow satin. I never saw it, yet at this moment, I feel that sensuous fabric swirl over my hot skin like the sea. . . . Then the fever breaks in a release of moisture, and I am lying on mangled, sour-smelling bedsheets.

Although Varina bristles whenever I'm referred to as a spinster, at thirty-four, I am comfortable with the designation. The title I have never been at ease with, "The Daughter of the Confederacy," was bestowed at a Lost Cause rally in late April 1886, two months before my twenty-second birthday. The harsh years of Reconstruction and the reign of the Northern carpetbaggers had ended; the South was starting to emerge from poverty, or at least to be optimistic that it could, and my father had become a sought-after speaker at agrarian fairs and Confederate veterans' reunions. I was accompanying him on a tour of commemorative events in Alabama and Georgia. (My mother and sister had to back out at the last minute, when Maggie's young son came down with scarlet fever.) As we arrived in Montgomery for the twenty-fifth anniversary of his inauguration there, a set piece of fireworks flashed the words "Welcome, Our Hero" in flaming letters. Our rooms at the Exchange Hotel were filled with roses—not only in vases and standing sprays, but in loose batches on the floor and furniture, as though they'd been flung from heaven. I had gathered up a few stems when I felt the sharp pricks of thorns. Jeff pressed his handkerchief on the drops of blood. "They look like rubies," he said. Then, his voice suffused with sadness, "The blood shed then would have made a river."

We were driven in a decorated carriage to the domed state house where, a quarter of a century earlier, he had taken the oath of office as Provisional President of the Confederate States of America. As requested, we had brought a cache of family trinkets and books to place in the cornerstone of a monument to be erected in memory of Alabamians who died in the War.

A local dignitary described the proposed structure, which would emanate from a base shaped like a Greek cross. Each arm of the cross would support a life-sized statue representing a branch of military service; from the center, a single round column would rise seventy feet to a Corinthian cap, on which would stand a ten-foot-tall bronze sculpture of a feminine figure representing Patriotism. When a member of the Ladies' Memorial Association, the major fund-raisers for the project, questioned the decision to have a female as the central, largest feature of a monument intended to honor men who had given their lives on battlefields, the New York sculptor explained that a male figure would not be architecturally or symbolically appropriate for that spot.

Jeff and I were seated close together on the front row of the platform, his arm draped possessively around my shoulder. His beard brushed my cheek like feathers as he whispered, "Well, then, my beautiful girl should be the model for that figure." They couldn't have heard, but the spectators on the wide front lawn of the Alabama State House smiled indulgently at their hero and the daughter who, they might have deduced from that display of affectionate, bantering closeness, lived to please him. I silently rationalized: Being in Montgomery, Alabama, where he was still held in high esteem, had triggered a rush of his former confidence and vigor; he had a need to flaunt these qualities to someone of the opposite sex, and I was handily available. My face was aflame with embarrassment. Yet when my father left my side to go to the podium a few feet away (he spoke that day with unusual animation and jollity), I felt his absence as keenly as though he had galloped off on his horse.

His burst of energy during the Montgomery celebration was short-lived. When the train made its scheduled stop at West Point, Georgia, Jeff did not feel up to greeting the assembly at the station. I was asked by our official escort, General Gordon, to accompany him in my father's stead to the rear of the train. As the crowd moved forward like a lumbering beast toward the railing of the caboose, the general announced, "Our chieftain is not able to greet you today, but it is my pleasure to introduce to you President Davis's youngest child, who was born toward the end of our great stand. Ladies and Gentlemen, here is Miss Winnie Davis, his and our daughter of the Confederacy."

It was ominously clear that the first letter of the word "daughter" was intended to be capitalized from then on. Biscuit-shaped caps the color of thunderclouds were hurled into the air as a great unison roar of the animalistic Rebel Yell caused my ears to ring and the small platform beneath me to shake alarmingly.

At that moment, what I previously had not allowed myself to comprehend struck me full-force: Jefferson Davis was the embedded anchor of the failed Secession. He had not been in favor of the nation's disintegration, but he had never wavered from his belief in the Constitutional rights of the States. In his words, "The government has no inherent power; all it possesses was delegated by the States"; therefore, since the Federal body had encroached upon these rights, the division into two separate nations was legal.

I was gone during the years he worked on his detailed, defensive treatise, *The Rise and Fall of the Confederate Government.* Reading the two-volume opus after I returned from Germany, I felt distanced from his premise and those cataclysmic events almost as though they were ancient history—yet I was painfully aware, whenever I turned a page, that this man had been far more vilified than any other leader of the vanquished South. I made a silent vow to stay close to him in public and extend my hand for clasping to spare his. By the time that itinerary, which included Atlanta and Savannah, was completed, my right hand was too swollen to fit into a glove. Wherever the festooned train made stops, children tossed white flowers onto the tracks, women kissed him and threw their arms around him (some fainted at the sight of him), and strong men wept. Usually reserved, during these demonstrations that were balm to his wounded spirit, Jeff was warmly outgoing and approachable. I did not try to emulate his example. I was learning to mentally separate from my new persona and the misdirected devotion it attracted.

According to the *Atlanta Constitution*, that city had never had such a "host within her borders, who came from a score of states, including those of the far North, to do honor to the revered

President." As we boarded the special car (with silver baskets of flowers suspended from the ceiling, and a Pullman berth for my father to rest on) for the trip to Savannah, I wished my mother or Maggie had been there to take my place on those stages. Either of them would have greeted the crowds with aplomb, while I was like a wooden marionette without strings.

A few months later, while staying with Connie and Burton Harrison in New York, I was invited by other friends of my parents to be their houseguest in Syracuse. I accepted because I had in mind submitting an article to the excellent *North American Review* at Cornell University, which I thought (erroneously, as it turned out) was located in that city. The possibility that I might fall in love there never occurred to me. That was supposed to happen in New Orleans.

When the first rumbles of disapproval about my romance with Fred Wilkinson reached us—what Varina called whispers behind the fans—Jeff said we should ignore them. But Jeff had died before the furor gathered steam. Some months ago, a reporter at the *World* handed me a clipping he had come across in another publication, which began: "Ask any Southerner of fifty or older, and he or she will state unequivocally that Winnie Davis, the favorite child of the late president of the Confederacy, willingly sacrificed her personal happiness rather than dishonor the Lost Cause by wedding the grandson of a notorious Abolitionist. . . ." After I read that far, I returned the clipping to him without comment.

My colleague said, "You must have seen a lot of testimonials on this subject."

"There are no testimonials, only gossip and speculation."

"We could set the record straight about you and your Yankee boy friend. Even make it up, if you'd rather not tell it like it was. What do you say we collaborate on a story that will satisfy them and—"

"I say no. Please respect my wishes, and do not bring up the subject to me again."

"Well, aren't you the princess," he muttered.

Varina's *Memoir* of her husband, which she wrote in an impassioned frenzy after he died, is more readable than his own. Critics have claimed that she had dates and facts wrong and that she was too blindly devoted to the man to see his shortcomings. They were wrong in the latter assumption. More than anyone else, his wife was acutely aware of Jeff's faults, not the least of which were his innate stubbornness and inability to compromise—but she was, and still is, determined to present him in the best possible light. My fear is that, should I die before my mother, she will write my life's story or anoint another to do so under her direction, and that her clever, glib manipulation of that particular topic, my thwarted happiness, will reflect her and me in a better light than either of us deserves.

In letters, travel logs, and diaries I kept as a young girl, I would write as though my mother were looking over my shoulder. I do not want her to know of, much less read, this collection of personal reminiscence and speculative analysis that I began a few months ago, after I returned from Egypt. The prudent part of me wants the outpouring destroyed before I leave this earth, yet another part of me does not concur. I keep the notebook hidden in the New York apartment and in this suite, in places too low for her to reach. I almost took it with me to Atlanta, and am glad

I didn't, as V. would have found it when she unpacked my suitcase. Fortunately, Kate has just been here and done my bidding
without asking questions. Her calming, cheerful presence in this
room over the last hour or so (although some of that time I was
asleep) has reinvigorated me.

V. had coaxed a spoonful of the doctor's medicine and one of
her own nostrums (celery juice, for nerves) down my throat,
brushed my unruly mop of hair, damp-sponged and powdered
my body, which in sickness cowers like a dog not allowed in the
house, dabbed my temples with her favorite rosewater cologne,
which is more acerbic than floral, and exchanged my crumpled,
perspiration-soaked nightgown for a fresh one. Then she went to
her room to make herself presentable for callers. She thrives on
being with people if they're not antagonistic to her. The Marl-
borough Hotel, where we lived when we first came to New York,
made a parlor available for her Sunday salons, which gathered
actors, artists, writers, and politicians. After we moved to the
Gerard, that management offered the same privilege. Had it not,
she would have found a hotel that did. Varina has a gift for bargaining.

Although here the routine is quite informal, the social custom
of paying calls is observed. As word gets about that one of us is
ailing, Varina's wide-ranging circle of acquaintances among the
summer colony at Narragansett Pier will bring flowers, fruit, tins
of confections and special teas, and morally uplifting books and
tracts.

Raising my body to a sitting position is not difficult. What is, is
convincing it not to continue rising. During the night just past, I
awoke with a sensation of levitation, as an apparition of a young

woman with hair as black as a starling's wing, an unusually wide forehead, and eyes like a spaniel's floated alongside me. I recognized Sarah Knox Taylor from the only portrait Jeff had of his first wife, whose father had been his commanding officer at Fort Crawford. Lieutenant Colonel Zachary Taylor had not approved of the courtship between his daughter and the handsome young dragoon; he wanted his delicate, beautiful child to have a gentler life than military encampments provided. I have also read that the colonel objected to Jefferson Davis's reputation for engaging in occasional wild exploits. But Jeff was determined; eventually, he resigned from the army, married Knox, and became a planter. Less than three months later, on a visit to his sister's Louisiana plantation, they both fell ill with malaria. Jeff survived, but Knox died and was buried there. When Jeff was elected to the United States Senate from Mississippi, his former father-in-law was President of the United States. The two men became close friends in Washington; so close, in fact, that President Zachary Taylor let it be known he regarded Jeff as a member of his family.

The phantom Knox dissolved when V. placed a folded, damp cloth on my brow and said, "Try not to thrash about, Winnie. Conserve your strength. We will ride this out."

In the sporadic intervals when my sister and I lived under the same roof, she entertained me with stories about the fortnightly socials our mother had held in the Richmond White House. The guest lists included officials of the separatist government and their wives, men from the nearby military camps, and prominent citizens of the Virginia city. Maggie and the boys watched from a curving staircase as the adults played charades and danced to the music of a fiddle and piano. After a sumptuous dinner—beefsteak pie and baked oysters were among her specialties—she would play matchmaker by herding bachelors and unmarried ladies into a parlor together. Later, when General Grant's forces were closing in on the Confederate capital, she would greet her guests with defiant aplomb in a taffeta gown that rustled like fire despite its patches, at "starvation parties," where there was little or no refreshment other than water. Robert Brown, their long-time servant, recalled that, near the end, his mistress bartered some of her jewelry for a scrawny turkey and a basket of near-rotten potatoes and carrots, which she stretched into a fricassee to feed fifty. The rustling-taffeta vision of Varina is among the clearest of my borrowed visions.

Jeff Jr.'s dramatic accounts of little Joe's fall to his death from the Executive Mansion's piazza seven weeks before I was born and of the family's exodus through the Carolinas into the Georgia woods have spawned images that are now so familiar they are no longer the stuff of nightmares. Maggie admonished me: "When Joe died, our parents were in deep grief over the loss of another boy. Having you brought some sunshine back to their faces, Pie. You must try never to disappoint them." At the time, we were on an ocean liner headed for England, where our father would look into an opportunity to make a living. A few weeks before, on my fourth birthday, he was carrying me when he fell down a flight of stairs in a hotel in Lennoxville, Quebec. Jeff suffered a concussion and two broken ribs, but he had managed to deposit me on a landing. "It's a damned miracle you weren't hurt, too," said thirteen-year-old Maggie, who had learned to swear on the streets of Richmond.

After our father was captured, Varina dispatched Maggie, Jeff Jr., and Willie to Canada in the care of her mother and sister, both named Margaret Howell, and Robert Brown. V. kept me with her in Savannah, where we lived under Federal guard in a hotel. Having used an anonymous gift of money to send the others out of the country, she had to pay for our lodging from her limited purse. Determined to save her husband, Varina wrote letters to influential Northerners who were sympathetic toward the plight of the leader of the Confederacy. Among those who volunteered to offer money for his release were industrialist Cornelius Vanderbilt, newspaper publisher Horace Greeley, and the outspoken Abolitionist Gerrit Smith. As a military prisoner, Jeff was deemed ineligible for bail. The accusation that the President of the Confederacy had been involved in the plot to murder President Lincoln had not held up; the charge that remained, treason, was a civil offense; therefore, the Virginia authorities could have demanded he be turned over to them. Presumably, this did not happen because security was stronger at the military prison than it would be in a state facility.

President Andrew Johnson had issued amnesties for almost all of the men who had fought for the South, and all could apply for pardons (which my father refused to do; he could not recant his convictions). None of the South's military leaders were still incarcerated; the former Vice President of the Confederacy, Alexander Stephens, had been freed; and the only two cabinet members still in custody had been scheduled for pardon. Public sentiment noted this scapegoating of one particular man, and even the Union Army's most ferocious general, William Tecumseh Sherman, is said to have conceded, "It would have been far better for everyone if Jefferson Davis had escaped."

The humanitarian effort initiated on my father's behalf would have allowed his children to visit him at Fort Monroe. He had given his consent for Varina to bring me with her, but not the others, because "they are old enough to form impressions. I could not bear for my boys to harbor, for the rest of their lives, a memory of seeing their father in chains, and behind bars."

After the losses of two young sons, he would not have guessed the lives of the remaining two would be snuffed out long before his own. Nor would my father have realized that I would absorb what I witnessed through infantile eyes and, as a young child, heard about that time when hatred and defamation mantled the defeated South—and that during my lonely exile in Germany, numbed by homesickness his affectionate letters brought on and were the antidote to, I would call forth these images to keep me company.

When I told Maggie our brother Joe used to come through a wall to visit me in Karlsruhe, not solid but with a bloom of life about him, she said I must never let on to our mother that her favorite of the six children she had given birth to was an earthbound ghost; it would kill her for sure. But it wouldn't have. Varina is amazingly resilient.

The morning's earliest replay: The doctor and Mr. and Mrs. Burns are here. A maid is leaving with a tray on which I see but do not hear dishes rattling. There is a taste of soft-boiled egg in my mouth. The scene—my view is from near the ceiling—appears as pantomime: The doctor's pink-and-white head moves from side to side and up and down; his hands wave as if he is conducting a chamber orchestra. The next time I open my eyes, everyone's gone but V., who is unpacking my larger suitcase and examining—sniffing, even—the contents to decide what should go into the laundry hamper. She sighs when she gets to the ruined gown.

A curlicued porcelain clock on the bedside table ticks impor-
tantly, as if to remind me of an appointment or that my allotment
of time on earth is ebbing.

It is now my favorite time of day. On this golden, New England
afternoon in Narragansett Pier, the sun will be benevolent, the
clear-as-a-jewel water cold and bracing. On the Mississippi Gulf
Coast, the sun would be full-tilt ablaze, the pigeon-colored surf
as warm and enticing as an embrace. "I want to go bathing," I say
tentatively, knowing from experience that infirmity negates free
will. The table is turned when V. suffers with angina, palpitations,
or pleurisy. Then I am in charge, and should I choose, can deny
her sherry and chocolates. She seems to enjoy the occasional
relinquishment of control, which may remind her of the way her
marriage was conducted. In spite of the man's difficult, controlling disposition, she loved her husband above all else, and does
so still. That kind of love would wear out some women, but she
draws strength from it. I wonder if he's youthful in her dreams,
as he often is in mine.

V. informs me briskly: "The doctor has ordered complete bed
rest for the rest of the week, with frequent ingestion of beef tea."

"That's a glum prospect. I'll slosh like a bucket."

"Here's one that should cheer you. I've sent a message to Kate
that you're indisposed, so it's quite likely she will be stopping by."
As she lifts my head to plump a pillow, pain slithers like a snake
from my forehead to the base of my skull. V. irritatingly tells me
what I had informed her of before I went to Atlanta, "The Pulitzers have leased a marble-floored mansion on Ocean Road."

"You shouldn't have bothered her."

"For heaven's sake, Winnie. Kate regards doing for us as her
pleasure. She and Joseph are proud of her blood relationship

with our family." V. has a remarkable sense of entitlement. She only pretends to scoff at being called Queen Varina. She seizes any opportunity to tell someone that babies, animals, ships, and a prison camp have been named for her. Mispronunciation of her name, so that it rhymes with vagina, infuriates her. "It's Va-REE-na," she corrects icily.

As to the blood relationship, I respond, "If such exists." Kate Pulitzer, whose maiden name is Davis, has never been specific as to how her line intersects with ours. I add, because I cannot resist, "Davis is one of the more common surnames."

"One thing that puts you off-kilter is your need to analyze."

While I'm deciding not to analyze that remark, she adds, "I'll be in my room, attending to correspondence. Ring the bell if you need me." Varina takes her letter writing seriously. Recipients who have known her long and well—Connie and Burton Harrison, who was Jeff's aide during the War and traveled with the family in those crucial days at the end; our Mississippi neighbors, Major Morgan and Judge and Mrs. Kimbrough; and when they were alive, the brilliant statesman Judah P. Benjamin, General Jubal Early, and V.'s clever, witty friend Mary Chesnut of South Carolina—have understood she expects these missives to be saved for posterity, even those that have scrawled across the envelopes "Private; please burn when read."

Granddaughter of a governor of New Jersey, daughter of a ne'er-do-well Natchez gentleman, wife of a former United States Senator and Secretary of War who gave up a Washington political career to head a band of rogue states, Varina Howell Davis is used to being snubbed and criticized in both North and South. Yet she has always held her head high. After the War, in the capitals of

Europe, she shrugged off the mantle of defeat and defection and was welcomed as though she were royalty.

She can be difficult, but she's fiercely loyal. The hollow whisper grazes my cheek like a soft, trimmed beard. Like my father's kiss.

Kate Pulitzer

AUGUST 3, 1898

We met Winnie Davis for the first time twelve years ago, at a party in Syracuse. My husband and I arrived a bit tardily and were informed by the host, "Our young friend from Mississippi is in the side parlor. She speaks fluent French and German, plays the piano on an artistic level, publishes literary works of remarkable erudition, and paints delightful landscapes."

Preoccupied as usual with his health and business concerns, Joseph had no idea who the guest of honor was. Perhaps I had neglected to tell him there was one. "With all those accomplishments, the miss from Mississippi should make a fine governess," he said grumpily as I led him toward the oval-faced girl who sat like a princess in an appropriately gilded chair. Winnie projects great physical charm. She has excellent posture and a rather athletic build. Taller than most women, she can meet a man's gaze on his level, although I am not sure that is an advantage for either, since she won't be deferential to him. Her face just misses being beautiful. Those large pewter-colored eyes are the best feature, and the symmetry is arresting; she has her father's patrician cheekbones. I especially approved of her gown in a rather daring shade of apricot that brought out the slightly golden cast of her complexion. I later learned the fabric had been a gift to her mother, who had it made up by one of those seamstresses who travel from house to house. Upper-class Southern women in reduced circumstances have a knack for making do in matters of style so that they and their daughters are never embarrassed by or feel they must apologize for their appearance.

I was happy to see Alfred Wilkinson, a personable young attorney whose family has been prominent in Syracuse since that city's founding, was keeping her company. "Good evening, Fred," I said. He bowed, having stood and all but clicked his heels together the moment he saw us approach. In the introduction, he cited her as "Miss Varina Anne Davis, who prefers to be called Winnie."

"What a charming nickname," I said, trying not to wince as she shook my hand with unnecessary firmness.

"Thank you." At least, she didn't talk like a man. Her voice was soft and melodious, and not particularly Southern in inflection. "According to my father, Winnie is an Indian word for 'bright and sunny.' He hoped it would guarantee me a happy disposition."

"And of course it did."

"Not entirely. I'm prone to occasional spells of gloom." The shadow that flickered across her face was quickly dispelled by a smile.

"Who is your father?" Joseph asked, despite my having reminded him, just before we arrived, not to press people he's barely met about their credentials.

"Jefferson Davis, sir, of Mississippi." She looked as if she expected to be reprimanded.

He beamed and clasped her hands so firmly I feared he might swing her about. "The President of the Southern Confederacy! You are that remarkable man's daughter?"

"Yes, Mr. Pulitzer."

"Please call me Joseph. And of course my youthful Kate will not have you calling her Mrs. or Madam. My dear, I have long admired your eminent father and look forward to making his acquaintance on my next journey South."

There are times when I find myself figuratively sweeping up after my husband, but this was not one of them. I was especially proud of his kindness toward Winnie when I learned she had received less than gracious reception at an event the previous evening. There was no evidence of hostility at this affair, where most if not all the invited were aware that our hosts, Dr. Thomas Emory and his wife, had strong ties to the Jefferson Davises. Tom Emory's father and Mr. Davis had been classmates at West Point. During the War Between the States, the family allegiances were divided: General William Emory served in the Union Army; his son Tom, who was a student at the University of Virginia when that state seceded, joined the Army of the Confederacy. General Emory's wife, a great-granddaughter of Benjamin Franklin, and Mrs. Davis were close friends in Washington when Mr. Davis was in the Senate, and also when he was a member of President Pierce's cabinet.

Winnie behaved with perfect decorum. She knew how to hold more than one man's attention at a time without making a spectacle of herself. She did not allow Fred Wilkinson to monopolize her that evening, although she encouraged him with the wiles of a natural belle: Her gloved hand would alight briefly on his arm; she would put a question to him and give him her full concentration as he answered. Joseph formed a different impression. If he had judged her to be even slightly a femme fatale who knew how to manipulate a man to advance her own purposes, he would not have said to me, just after we took our leave that evening, that I should cultivate Miss Winnie Davis as a matter of family courtesy.

"Family courtesy?" I repeated. "I don't believe I've heard that expression before." My Hungarian-bred husband, who learned English after he arrived in America at the age of seventeen, would rather invent an idiom than search for one.

"She shares your maiden name. As your blood kin, she is entitled to your patronage and affection."

I had a vision of hundreds of children peeping out of mountain cabins, claiming to be my cousins. "I don't believe I have heard my father mention a family connection to Mr. Jefferson Davis."

"However, as the judge is a native of the Commonwealth of Virginia, he would not object to having the Rebel chief as a relative, would he?"

The notion did seem interesting. "Darling, I shall do my best to see Winnie again before she leaves the vicinity and assure her that we are utterly at her disposal."

Joseph kissed my chin quite thoroughly, although he had aimed for my mouth. "I am drawn to the plight of this young lady," he said. "Even with my poor eyes, I can see a desperation in hers. I hope she is spirited enough to transcend the tragedy she was born into. I should like her to know we are available to come to her aid whenever and however she might need us."

The next day, I sent orchids to Winnie Davis with an invitation to tea, which she accepted by messengered note. I could tell she was pleased that there would be just the two of us. It was also obvious that she could become as engrossed in conversation with another woman as with someone of the opposite sex. The interchange had hardly begun when I intuitively knew we would become true friends who would never be rivals. As I drew her out on a variety of subjects, she responded thoughtfully, but not as though she were trying to impress me. The single off-putting thing about Winnie, I soon discovered, was that any chair she sat upon became a throne, no matter how ordinary her attire or how helter-skelter her hair might appear. When I met her mother, who could be a twin to Queen Victoria, and her father, who brought to mind a picture-book illustration of the legendary King Arthur, I realized Winnie came by the regal posturing naturally.

During that tête-à-tête at our residence on Thirty-fifth Street, she spoke little about her life abroad as a young girl, but enough to let me know that she had relished a summer in Paris after several years at a Protestant boarding school in Germany. Later, in an article for the *Ladies' Home Journal*, she would write forcefully about the deleterious effects of foreign education on young girls.

Perhaps Winnie seemed to take to me immediately because I am near the age of her only sister, Maggie Hayes, whom she does not get to see as often as she would like. When Maggie and her husband lived in Memphis, they and their children visited frequently at Beauvoir. Although Mrs. Davis claims the move to Colorado Springs was due to her son-in-law's weak lungs, I suspect Addison Hayes wanted to be his own man, which must have been difficult while he lived within convenient proximity of in-laws who were used to having people at their beck and call.

As we were getting to know each other, when Winnie remarked that most young women of her acquaintance were superficial and flighty, I confessed, "Except for the young part, you've just summed me up. I cannot think of a single thing I've ever been serious about. I do not have a talent for any of the arts."

She said, "You have cultivated the art of being pleasant. You radiate goodwill, Kate. People can't help but find pleasure in your company."

"Heavens. That's the nicest accolade I've ever had from one of my own gender." After I realized it would never occur to her to play up to anyone, I valued the compliment even more. Although she graciously accepts items from my wardrobe, Winnie refuses to let me treat her to a new garment or bauble. She does not share my obsession with fashion and adornment, and she's aware that the allowance Joseph keeps me on does not always cover my extravagant impulses.

Soon after we became acquainted with Winnie, a correspondence ensued between Joseph and her parents, in which Mrs. Davis participated with enthusiasm. My husband was impressed by the woman's vigorous intellect, and after he came to know her, by a personality as forceful and flamboyant as his own. The meeting took place in January 1888, when Joseph routed us to California through New Orleans. "There we will take a detour to a Mississippi village called Biloxi, which is near the Davis estate," he announced, when he informed me of the plans to cross the country by private train. To accommodate the Davises and their frequent visitors, the Louisville & Nashville Railroad had installed a section of track with a flag stop along the backside of their property. It was not unusual for visitors to find their hosts seated on a fallen tree trunk, awaiting their arrival. Shortly before we were due to arrive at the Davises' picturesque, rather dilapidated house-by-the-sea, I reminded Joseph again that we must not mention Fred Wilkinson, as Winnie had not yet informed her parents of the romance that had flourished through correspondence and her visits to New York.

While she was our houseguest the previous August, we did everything we could think of to fan the flame. Joseph was convinced an alliance between the President of the Confederacy's daughter and the grandson of the celebrated New Englander Samuel May, a founder of the American Abolitionist Society and an associate of Emerson, Longfellow, and Lowell, would help put to rest the still-smoldering hostility between North and South. As a new arrival to this country during the last year of the War, my husband had served in the back ranks of the Union Army's First New York Lincoln Cavalry, which took part in General William Tecumseh Sherman's infamous path of destruction through Georgia and other Southern states. Joseph does not talk about his military experiences, but over the years following the conflict, he developed great respect and empathy for Jefferson Davis, the South's standard-bearer. By the time they met, each was almost blind in one eye.

Winnie's father is a sacred symbol for devotees of the Lost Cause, but he's also been the subject of some rascally rumors, not all of which originated in the North. One is that he seduced Mrs. Sarah Dorsey, a well-to-do widow who died of cancer (he was at her bedside in the New Orleans hospital), into bequeathing to him her entire estate, including land in Louisiana and Arkansas as well as the oceanfront acreage in Mississippi. Mrs. Davis told my husband the former properties had been entailed by mortgages and the latter, which President Davis subsequently left in his will to Winnie, had become an albatross. According to her mother, Winnie has turned down an offer of $90,000 for Beauvoir, because the prospective buyers would have made a resort of the place. Both women envision its becoming a rest home for old Confederate soldiers and a shrine to Jefferson Davis. Joseph thinks the notion is impractical but he admires the idealism.

Winnie did not go with us to California at that time, but she's accompanied us on several other junkets. The most recent, this past winter, was an extensive stay in Egypt, where she attended lectures, climbed pyramids, and would have embarked on a field study caravan with camel-riding explorers, all of whom were men, had we not advised her that would be unseemly. Joseph sternly reminded Winnie that she was not his intrepid reporter Nellie Bly, who several years ago had talked him into letting her attempt to match or best the record illustrated in Jules Verne's popular book *Around the World in Eighty Days*. (Over a million people entered the contest, which was Joseph's idea, to guess the time it would take Nellie to circle the planet. As it turned out, she surpassed the eighty-day benchmark with a tally of seventy-two days, six hours, eleven minutes, and fourteen seconds.) I could see that my husband's remark struck a nerve. Winnie would thrive on a real journalistic career, but she does not have the freedom, nor the stamina, to pursue such a path. Prior to embarking on the Egyptian tour, she had nursed her mother through a spell of heart failure that lasted most of the winter. Yet paradoxically, even as she becomes increasingly reliant on her daughter, Mrs. Davis encourages Winnie to stretch her wings at every opportunity.

I was remiss in not calling on them at the Rockingham until a week after Winnie returned from one of those veterans' conventions that deplete her energy. My husband had learned, probably from asking her directly, that Winnie has received honorariums for lending her presence to these events, in addition to having her expenses covered. And he has it from "reliable sources" that Mrs. Davis, as soon as she became First Lady of the Confederacy, talked railway and steamship lines into providing complimentary transportation for her and other members of the family. Apparently, those arrangements are still in effect.

According to the publicity, this latest commemoration of the Lost Cause brought twenty thousand War veterans and their wives, plus at least two thousand spectators, to Atlanta's Exposition Park. In addition to the public events, hundreds of the city's private homes hosted glittering receptions and cotillions. Of all the notable personalities attending the festivities, Winnie was given top billing, as though she were a famous actress or opera singer or, as in the slant of one journalist, a canonized saint. From the tone and content of Mrs. Davis's note, I discerned that she blames the Confederate States of America Veterans' Association, the city of Atlanta, the state of Georgia, and the widow of one of the South's greatest hero-generals for Winnie's current malaise: "My poor child, soaked to the skin by a downpour in all that oppressive heat, could not get out of the congestion to return to her hotel and change clothes. I was informed that Winnie insisted on keeping to her travel schedule, although clearly she was too ill to leave, and that Mrs. Thomas 'Stonewall' Jackson, who had ridden in the same carriage with her, was not adversely affected by the weather. Apparently, Mary Anna Jackson had the forethought to bring a sturdy umbrella but not the generosity to share it. Winnie's flimsy sunshade disintegrated when the first shards of rain hit it. . . ."

I should have come early this morning, as soon as I got the message, but I have had a busy summer here, being hostess to a steady infusion of newspaper executives summoned by Joseph for lessons in economy. For the past twelve months the paper has had its largest circulation ever, yet is steadily losing money. My husband's asthma and diabetes are directly affected whenever something goes awry with that publication, and the ongoing rivalry with the impossible ogre Mr. William Randolph Hearst keeps things stirred up.

When I arrived at their rooms, Mrs. Davis whispered, "She's just dropped off to sleep. Winnie has extremely restless nights and is not responding significantly to treatment prescribed by the doctor or to my own tried-and-true ministrations. Kate, you've seen her at her absolute worst; she won't mind if you peep in at her now. I would value your opinion as to the state of her health."

I should, indeed, have some expertise in that area, as my husband is a chronic semi-invalid, and I care for him with compassion and diligence. However, I tend not to dwell on what is long-standing in his condition that I can do nothing about, such as extreme pallor, bloodshot eyes, and occasional twitching of limbs. I love Joseph and Winnie, but they are both so neurotic it is difficult to distinguish between what is brought on by physical debilitation and what comes from their agitated states of mind. "I would of course like to see her," I said. "I'll sit quietly by and not wake her."

Mrs. Davis took me to Winnie's room, and to my relief, did not come in with me. The woman has presence as great as her girth, and Winnie best comes into her own when her mother is not on the scene. Partially open windows admitted a heavenly sea breeze, but neither that nor the fragrance of lilies I had brought to her could dispel the pervasive odor of vomit. Winnie lay quite still, her face all but submerged in a nest of abundant wavy hair the color of maple syrup, or fine cognac. Deep mauve shadows circled her closed eyes. She did not appear to be breathing. Waiting for her to wake up, I relived the sadness of last January, at Chatswold, our residence at Bar Harbor, when my seventeen-year-old Lucille succumbed to a virulent attack of typhoid fever. Neither Joseph nor I could bear to return, less than a year later, to the Maine resort where our beautiful child was taken from us soon after her coming-out party. That is how we happened to be spending this summer at Narragansett Pier, which began as a freight wharf for farmers to ship their goods off to Providence. Since the construction a few years ago of the Narragansett Towers and Casino, designed by the architects McKim, Mead, and White, the village has become a popular beach colony resort for upper-middle-class people. There's much more to do and see in this area now. I would love to take Winnie for a drive along Ocean Road, then to luncheon at the casino or the new country club at Point Judith; she likes to see the lighthouse up close. . . . It's rotten luck that she has to languish inside when the weather and scenery are so lovely.

Forgetting I was not to wake her, I said, "Winnie, please tell me you're all right."

"Kate. I'm glad you're here." Her eyelids flickered but did not stay open. She murmured drowsily, "I don't know that I'm all right, or right at all. This may be the real thing."

As far as I knew, Winnie did not attend séances, but she put stock in prophetic omen. She had told me of ghastly death dreams, of seeing herself in a casket. "No, it's not," I said firmly. "You have been far sicker before. Do you remember that time in Naples—"

"How could I forget! That was when I showed Fred my true colors."

Albeit a topic that I would have enjoyed exploring with her, this was not the time to get into it. I was surprised to hear her speak his name; usually she would turn stonily silent when anyone else did. "I meant you gave us a terrible scare then, but much to our relief and surprise, you pulled through quite dramatically."

"You pulled me through. Now you must do me a simpler favor."

"Anything."

"In the foyer, on the bottom shelf of the bookcase by the door, there's a set of dark blue books with illegibly faded titles—not ours, they're part of the furnishings. Tucked out of sight behind them is a binder I would like you to bring to me. I do not wish my mother to know of its existence."

"What if she catches me rummaging around?"

"Could you offer to stay with me for awhile, so she can go out?"

"Of course. I'll make the suggestion." I was sorry I had not thought to do that as soon as I arrived. Mrs. Davis, poor haggard old thing, was thrilled to be relieved. She scurried off to freshen up.

I had brought a blancmange made by our excellent cook. Winnie let me spoon in a few mouthfuls, then said, "That's all I can hold. I can't keep much of anything down. Kate, how can you stand to be around me?"

The first response that came to mind would have been too hurtful: *Because being around you makes me aware of my own good fortune. I have a husband I adore and admire, who treasures me, and there are no weighty issues complicating my mind, like whether my father was responsible for the bloodiest war in history, and how dishonorably he was treated in comparison to other prominent leaders of the defeated*

South. . . . So I said the next thing: "Because you are not like the other women I know. You're complex and amazing, but never irritating or overbearing, and you are very dear to me." There was enough truth in that declaration to cause tears to form in my eyes and hers.

"And you are very dear to me, and we sound like a couple of geese." She added defiantly, as though she expected me to refute the statement, "I was not cut out for marriage."

At that moment, wearing a heavier shawl than was called for and a previous year's bonnet with the most dejected-looking ribbons imaginable, Mrs. Davis reappeared and said in the smooth contralto that can spin out, according to her whim, delightfully droll, deeply perceptive, or preposterously tactless remarks, "Darling, I'm sure Kate will agree with me: Intelligent women never think they are cut out for marriage."

It's just as well she did not press me for corroboration. I would have said, "On the contrary, from the time I was seven years old, my one ambition in life was to be married." I might have added: *. . . to an exciting, driven man who would create an empire and become wealthy beyond my wildest expectations. I conjured him in my dreams, then waited for him to find me, and he did. . . .*

I accompanied Mrs. Davis to the outer door, and as soon as she had departed, located the object Winnie had requested and dusted it off with my petticoat before bringing it to her. She gathered the thing to her as she might have a child or a puppy. (Winnie is wonderful with animals and children.) She said—whispered almost; her voice was weaker than I'd ever heard it before—"While I'm laid up, I can revisit these scrawled pages. The new hiding place will be beneath this bed, which I can manage. Kate, this is important: If I should die here, or if it looks like I'm going into a twilight state, please retrieve this notebook immediately, and take it away with you. I don't want it be found by someone who would turn it over to my mother. I won't ask you not to read what I've written here, but please do wait until I've really gone, and then destroy it."

"The next place you're really going is somewhere wonderful with us." I disdained to address the rest of that sentence. The presumption that I would be inclined to read her journal must have been due to the illness. Winnie was well aware that my taste in pastimes runs to shopping for clothes, millinery, jewelry, and objets d'art; dining in exquisite surroundings; and attending the theatre, light opera, museums and galleries, balls, receptions, and occasional séances. Of course, I have read her pretty book, *The Veiled Doctor* (which has a stylish peacock imprinted in gold on a grass-green cover), and I look forward to the new novel—but perusing handwritten text in a pasteboard-backed tablet would be like overseeing the children's schoolwork, a task best left to those trained for it.

She had drifted back into sleep. Her lips moved slightly and she moaned as though making love in a dream. I fervently hoped she was. I recalled when her face was flushed, not with illness, but with pleasure, because Fred Wilkinson was around. But she never showed any inclination to take me into her confidence about why a love affair that seemed like an ideal match had ended, and so acrimoniously. When Fred came to Naples to console her after her father died, I should have been more observant, but I did not regard myself as their chaperone; Winnie was twenty-five years old and the man had every intention of marrying her.

Upset by the rumbles in the Deep South over her romance with a Northerner, Winnie had welcomed the opportunity to sail with us to Paris that November on Joseph's soundproof yacht. Except for my husband's complaints about noise—as his eyesight failed, his hearing became so acute that any loud sound caused him pain—we were having a pleasant sojourn. Then, in early December, word came that Mr. Davis had died. Her mother wired instructions that Winnie was to remain abroad with us, since she could not get back in time for the funeral. Stricken with grief— she had adored her father—Winnie sank into a spiraling depression. By early spring, I decided a change of scenery would be beneficial for both Winnie and Joseph. We sailed south to Naples and the Grand Hotel. The entourage included a newly hired editor at the *World*, our children, several servants, one of Joseph's physicians, and the ubiquitous flock of secretaries he must have available at all times.

Unfortunately, nature, both God's and my husband's, conspired against what should have been an idyllic interlude. The weather was terrible, and there were explosions in the nearby bay, where cannon was being tested. Joseph had dispatched messages to the Italian Minister of War to stop the unbearable noise immediately, but the testing had not ceased altogether. Winnie showed a bit of her usual spunk when she asked Joseph how he could distinguish cannon blasts from the sound of waves crashing against the seawall. I was delighted when Fred Wilkinson, at the nudging of Mrs. Davis, came to Naples to join us. After he arrived, Winnie eventually perked up and the lovers went about on their own. They saw the ruins of Pompeii and traveled up Vesuvius. However, Winnie informed me later that the rains had kept them inside the inn for much of that latter excursion.

The melancholia brought on by her painful loss seemed to abate while Fred was present. He was able to continue on to

Rome with our party, but could not remain with us indefinitely; he had to return to the business of earning a livelihood. On the day he bade me good-bye, Fred seemed quite subdued, as if he were the one who had suffered a loss. At dinner a few hours later, I asked Winnie if she missed her sweetheart already. The question appeared to startle her. Then, "Oh, God, Kate. I miss my father," she said. I had never before heard such anguish in her voice. "I cannot believe he won't be there when I return." She began to weep quietly, yet visibly. Although Joseph, in conversation with his current protégé, appeared not to notice, I knew how he abhorred any disturbance at table—he will not tolerate what he calls "mewling" from the children—so I suggested to Winnie that we go to her stateroom. There I gave her a large dose of a strong-smelling sedative that had been provided by her mother and looked like boot polish. I had my maid come to help her get ready for bed. Winnie assured me she would be fine by morning, and indeed, when I next saw her some twelve hours later, she appeared to be collected and in better spirits. Although she made a conscious effort to put forth a cheerful countenance for the rest of the trip, she stayed in her quarters most of the time. I did not think that unusual, as Winnie loves to read, and she has disciplined herself to spend a good portion of each day writing. Also, burdened as she is with an intelligent and inquiring mind, she quite likely spends a lot of time in profound thought.

In April, soon after Fred left us, a formal notice of his engagement to Winnie was published. I was surprised by Mrs. Davis's having taken that step while Winnie was still abroad. By the time she returned home, a vehement protest over the Daughter of the Confederacy's betrothal to a man "not of the South" had erupted in letters to Fred in Syracuse, to Winnie and her mother in Mississippi, and to newspapers around the country. I heard—not from any of the parties directly involved—that Alfred Wilkinson was referred to in some of these communications as a "God-damned Yankee son-of-a-bitch."

Gossip also had it that Mrs. Davis had expected Fred to seize the moment and marry Winnie when he crossed the Atlantic to be with her after her father's death. Joseph commented, after I passed that morsel on to him, that if such were the case, Mrs. Davis's instincts were right. He wished he had thought to offer the *Liberty* for a shipboard ceremony and honeymoon cruise. The sheer romance of that kind of elopement would have put a damper on any potential furor and might have prevented Mrs. Davis's complaining to friends—and even to the young man himself—about Fred's inability to talk Winnie out of her depression.

Shortly after Winnie returned to Mississippi in midsummer, Fred's mother's house in Syracuse burned to the ground. The Wilkinsons' fine possessions, among them valuable paintings and statuary, and an elderly servant perished in the flames. In August, Mrs. Davis published a notice that the wedding had been postponed until late June 1891, with the explanation that Winnie did not wish to be married until a full year had elapsed since her father's death.

About the same time, a prominent gentleman from Mississippi was dispatched by Mrs. Davis to make inquiries in Syracuse about Fred's financial situation. Some scandal about his family was unearthed at that time, in addition to revelations that the Wilkinson wealth had been exhausted when the Wilkinson Brothers Bank suffered reversals some years before the fire consumed the house. Mrs. Davis and her snooping advisor speculated that

Fred's income would not be sufficient to support Winnie. In mid-October, during a visit by Fred to Beauvoir, he expressed to Mrs. Davis his resentment of her initiating that investigation. Shortly thereafter, he and Mrs. Davis acknowledged the ending of the engagement. Fred gallantly conceded the decision was the wish of Winnie and her mother; Mrs. Davis cited Winnie's poor health as the reason. The South claimed a victory as though it had been won on a battlefield: The Daughter of the Confederacy would not be carried off by the enemy.

From then on, the issue was treated by the principals—Winnie, her mother, and Fred—as a closed book. After the dust had settled a bit, Mrs. Davis contrived to have Winnie meet or become reacquainted with eligible suitors in New Orleans, Savannah, Charleston, Atlanta, and heaven knows how many more cities. From the time they moved to New York, I have arranged place cards at our gatherings so that Winnie is always seated next to or across from an unmarried gentleman. Well, not all may be gentlemen, but if they're at our table, they are capable of interesting conversation, which Winnie, like Joseph, requires. Her aura of self-containment intrigues some and discourages others, but she has not lacked for escorts. However, to my knowledge, she has not been enamored of anyone since Fred Wilkinson, and I have heard no rumor of a romantic attachment on his part, although it's quite likely he has had the kind that men keep secret.

A couple of years after the breakup, Joseph asked me to include both of them at the same dinner party.

"But darling, wouldn't that reignite the spark of scandal that surrounded their rift?" I protested.

"I doubt it. The people on this guest list have more to put their minds to than fanning a dead flame."

"Should I warn Winnie?"

"Warn her of what? That she will be dining with perceptive, stimulating people, among whom may be her former fiancé? Of course not. As a member of a family whose history is filled with strife and controversy, she must have weathered many more jarring experiences than our festive occasion would provide. I would expect both Wilkinson and Miss Davis to be completely civil and cordial to each other while they are our guests."

It did not turn out as Joseph predicted. Fred and Winnie almost collided before they spotted each other. According to an observer, each stared and turned pale at the sight of the other. Then like the swan she can be, Winnie sailed away into an adjacent parlor to insulate herself among people, furniture, and potted palms. Fred headed for the front door, stopping briefly to tell me he was not feeling well enough to stay for dinner. He politely declined the next invitation, and I don't believe we have had him on a list since, other than for Joseph's all-male gatherings. I do not recall running into him at any intimate social events, although I have glimpsed him at large affairs and on a few occasions with his sisters at the theatre and opera. One of the Wilkinson girls married, but the others are typical New England, gaunt-faced spinsters. Fred's name surfaces occasionally in news items relevant to his line of work; apparently he does quite well as a patent attorney. With so many marvelous things being invented these days, patents must be greatly in vogue.

I had been in that close, depressing room for over an hour. On the fern stand directly in my line of vision was a tarnished silver vase filled with peacock plumage; the iridescent orbs in those dusty feathers seemed to be staring at me. Winnie lay still as death except for the wisp of breath that made her chest rise and fall. It didn't appear she would wake anytime soon. I extracted the notebook she was anxious about from one of her large but delicately boned hands. As I knelt to place it beneath the bed frame, the plain blue cover fell open to reveal the first page's startling heading in her childlike penmanship: "My Father's Peccadilloes." Recalling that Joseph had been impressed with a piece Winnie wrote for the *Sunday World* in which she had extolled her father, and knowing how she idolized his memory, I could not imagine her acknowledging that the man had any faults, much less writing about them, even in a form not intended for publication.

Then, and again over the next days as Winnie alternated between getting well and sinking deeper into the abyss of her illness, that word *peccadilloes* reminded me of a ludicrous anecdote about Jefferson Davis. In a cartoon (which certainly did not run in my husband's newspaper; I forget how I came across it, and of course, I've never mentioned it to Winnie or her mother), he is shown scrambling down, his clothes in disarray, from an upper berth of a sleeping car. A glimpse beyond the parted curtain reveals the berth's occupant as a disheveled, buxom woman; no identity is provided. In the balloon caption, Mr. Davis informs the conductor: "This lady's husband asked me to see to her safety while she and I coincidentally happened to be traveling overnight on the same train."

While I was dreamily imagining the diatribe Mrs. Davis might have hurled at him after that humiliation, she returned to the sickroom and caught me about to nod off in a stiff, shinily upholstered slipper chair, the kind of appointment one encounters in hotels that put decor ahead of comfort. The Rockingham, the best of the ten or twelve hotels in Narragansett Pier, attracts clients who may not be able to afford first-class accommodations yet can impart a measure of prestige by their presence. Those Burnses are quite proud to have the Davis celebrities among their summer "regulars"; I suspect the rate is significantly reduced for them. Winnie remarked recently that this is the sixth summer they've been here. Maggie Hayes brought them the first time, when Mrs. Davis became so enamored with the resort. However, Winnie prefers Bar Harbor, where she first visited the Burton Harrisons and has often visited us. As I rose to leave the bedside watch, her mother said, "I've asked some of my friends to come a week from Friday at one o'clock to play cards. I hope Winnie will be able to go for an outing then."

I responded as she wished me to: "A drive and luncheon in a pleasant inn should do her a world of good. I'll come for her that morning about half past eleven."

I did not see them again until the appointed date. I had intended to send my chauffeur into the hotel to fetch Winnie, but decided that might appear high-handed. Their pleasant little New York maid opened the door to me. I was glad to see this young woman had been sent for, and was about to tell her so when Mrs. Davis appeared and said, "Oh, Kate, thank heaven you're here. Things have taken a turn. We haven't been able to get Winnie dressed. She's not keeping any food down now." I took one look at my friend, who was either asleep or unconscious, and hurried back to the lobby to place a telephone call to one of Joseph's physicians in New York. The man was there within hours. After listening through a stethoscope to the mysterious insides of Winnie's limp body, he said, "It appears Miss Davis has contracted malarial gastritis."

"Is that serious?" I asked.

He made the harrumphing noise doctors resort to when they don't know what to say, then blew his nose thoroughly into a handkerchief and examined the contents before replying, "It certainly can be. In order to get well, the patient must demonstrate she has the will to live."

"And how would she do that, in her debilitated state?" I persisted.

"She must be encouraged to eat and drink."

Mrs. Davis said, "Winnie cannot retain anything except an occasional spoon of egg white and small sips of lemonade."

"Well, do your best," he said, and patted her hand. "Mrs. Pulitzer will keep me informed."

My husband had informed me that morning that he was ready to return to the city. If the servants got everything packed, we would depart the next day. I waited until the doctor had left before telling Mrs. Davis, "I can come back at a moment's notice, so you must stay in touch." I pressed my cheek to hers and felt it quiver like a bird. "Try not to worry. We must think only life-affirming thoughts."

I remembered Winnie's instructions to me several weeks later, by which time Mrs. Davis was back in New York. I immediately contacted Mr. Burns at the Rockingham and explained that Winnie, as a writer for my husband's newspaper, had told me her current work was in a notebook that she kept beneath the bed in their suite; she had asked that I be sure to retrieve the folio in the event she was incapacitated. Mr. Burns replied rather huffily that no personal property of the Davises had been found in those rooms; Mrs. Davis had asked for packing boxes, and had left the place clean as a whistle.

If Winnie knows I failed miserably in the one thing she asked of me at the end of her life, I hope she also knows that Joseph and I gave her a dignified, tasteful send-off, with the finest casket and floral trimmings, and that I shall miss her terribly, and am resolved to be kindly attentive to her mother for the rest of that courageous woman's life, or mine.

Winnie's Notebook

MY FATHER'S PECCADILLOES

Four and a half years ago, a startling revelation came to me from
Prairie du Chien, Wisconsin. Labeled "Personal, to Miss Varina
Anne (Winnie) Davis, in care of the *New York World*," the letter was
forwarded to our home address. I slit the top of the plain, work-
manlike envelope and hoped the contents would not require a response. Unlike my mother, who replies with prompt civility even
to those who criticize something she has written or is purported
to have said or done, I prefer to put that time and energy on
writing for publication or, as in these private pages, on analyzing
events, people, and my own thoughts and impressions.

On that mid-January day in 1893, I had just returned to the
apartment from a satisfying walk through flurries of snow in
Central Park, where I imagined myself disappearing into that
spongy whiteness and dissolving with it into oblivion. For one
vaporizing, light-headed moment, it seemed I had achieved that
transition—that my hand on the doorknob, although still visible, was no longer corporeal, but as weightless as a moth. Yet
the door had opened, and at the sound of it, Margaret Connelly,
her pretty apple-shaped cheeks flushed with heat from the coal

grate and her Irish blood, hurried in from the kitchen to relieve me of my damp muff and cloak. I accepted her cheerful offer of a cup of tea and waited until Margaret had left the room again before opening the only mysterious communication in the stack of mail she had retrieved. The tiny fireplace glowed silently as I read the letter, then re-read it, until the penciled handwriting, with its exaggerated loops in *l*'s and *y*'s and curious marks like bird wings over the *i*'s, was as clear as if it were stamped on the wall opposite me. Since that day, the letter has been hidden in a glove box. Now it occurs to me how foolhardy that was. The more housebound V. becomes, the more she pries among my things. At least I know she hasn't come across it. If she had found Mr. Brown's letter, she would have mentioned it to me. Not merely mentioned. She would have screamed, *How could you have kept this slanderous lie from me?*

My calm retort would have infuriated her even more: *Because I do not believe it is a lie, and I did not want you to be hurt.*

12 January 1893

Dear Miss Davis:

By way of introduction, I am Edward J. Brown, a merchant and miller in Prairie du Chien, Wisconsin. The excellent newspaper you and your mother are associated with occasionally finds its way to our remote town. The articles with your name attached indicate you are a perceptive and compassionate young woman, as well as a gifted purveyor of words. Therefore, I am taking the liberty of writing to you on behalf of someone who can neither read nor write, yet is a most remarkable, intelligent fellow, and highly deserving, in my opinion, of some recognition from your family, especially now that he is over sixty years old. This man's name, Jeff Davis, is recorded in an old ledger from the early 1850s. It does not require a stretch of the imagination to see his strong resemblance to your late father, who as you may be aware, had military service in this area during the late 1820s to early '30s.

While posted at Fort Crawford, Lieutenant Jefferson Davis was sent farther east, to help build Fort Winnebago at the portage between the Fox and Wisconsin Rivers. The youthful officer was evidently highly thought of by his superiors, as he was put in charge of dismantling an illegally built sawmill. Lieutenant Davis worked so hard he took sick and almost died, and would have, so the legend goes, had it not been for an African manservant he'd brought with him from Mississippi, who cared for him and nursed him back to health. The Chippewas admired Lieutenant Davis and called him, with affection, "Little Chief," because he was eager to learn their language and ways. Soon, the strong, agile young white man could perform tribal dances and race horses with the best of the braves.

My dear Miss Davis, I heard stories, as a boy, about your father and other soldiers staging dog-and-wolf fights with the Indians, and one that persists hereabouts concerns Jefferson Davis's love for a beautiful tribal princess who bore his son. She died young, whether of a broken heart or of privations suffered by the natives due to the encroachment of white settlers, I could not say, but the latter hardship would be cause enough. Nor can I say with any certainty whether Lieutenant Davis was aware that he had left a child in these parts.

This boy, who was given your father's name, became known in the white settlement as "Indian Jeff." He was told he was born in 1831. For many years, he was an expert river man and trapper, but illness and the harsh winters hereabouts have impeded his ability to earn his way. Some of us other old-timers see to his welfare now. It occurred to me you might find it in your heart to send this Jeff Davis something that belonged to your father, and perhaps a lock of your hair. I gave him a carte de visite distributed by Dr. Harter's Medicine Co. of St. Louis, Missouri, which displays your lovely image above the caption "Winnie Davis, the Daughter of the Confederacy," and he was quite taken with it.

Respectfully yours,
Edward J. Brown

I sent Mr. Brown a package containing four ten-dollar bills, a meerschaum pipe and leather tobacco pouch, both of which had belonged to Jeff, and a wisp of my hair in an enameled, locket-size frame. It occurred to me to include a pearl-centered stickpin I had bought in Paris and given to my father the first Christmas I spent at Beauvoir (he had attached it to his ascot, then pressed my hand over the spot; the pearl had pulsated against my palm as though it were alive), but I decided that would be inappropriate, as a man of the wilderness would have no use for such an ornament.

Mr. Brown's prompt acknowledgment informed me the gifts were greatly appreciated. The lack of any "I hope to hear from you again" or "Your half-brother would like to make your acquaintance" phraseology did not surprise me, as the note I had enclosed in the package was brief and noncommittal. I could not welcome that Jeff Davis into the family; therefore, I should not express an interest in meeting him. Broad-minded as my mother is in most respects, she would prefer not to know of the existence of an illiterate, illegitimate stepson near her own age.

A few months later, I dispatched a twenty-dollar bill to Mr. Edward Brown with a card inscribed, "For J. Davis with continued best wishes from V. A. Davis." The still-sealed envelope was returned to me with the stamped notation "Addressee is Deceased." I had thought of making up a reason to travel to Wisconsin and of confiding this secret to Maggie, in the hope that she might go with me. When I learned the man who had written to me was no longer around to be the go-between, I took the easy way out and did nothing. I have never heard anything more from Wisconsin, but sometimes, on the fringe of sleep, I see two virile young men paddling a canoe on a river. One is my father. Except for a ruddier complexion, the other could be his twin. Neither is wearing clothing other than a loincloth. I wish I could ask the man I knew these questions: *When my mother wanted to give her second-born male infant your name, did you feel a twinge of guilt at not informing her you already had a namesake child? After that son dropped out of Virginia Military Institute with failing grades, did you wonder how your other offspring with the same name might have done with such an opportunity? When the brother I knew and loved died soon after attaining the age of manhood, and Varina sobbed, "God has taken all our boys," were you aware that you, at least, still had one?*

The African manservant Mr. Brown referred to in his letter was the slave James Pemberton, who was left to Jeff by his father, Samuel Davis. After Jeff graduated from West Point, Jim Pemberton accompanied him to his army post; later, Jeff made this man his overseer at Brierfield Plantation, and before the War began, offered him his freedom, but Jim declined to take it. If

Jeff had left a son in that wilderness, Jim Pemberton would have been aware of it, and would have taken the secret to his grave. There was only one other I could think of who possibly would know the true story. William Harney, who had been stationed at Fort Crawford with my father, had come to Beauvoir on several occasions. After dinner, Mr. Harney and my father would go out to the porch, to sit in the dark together. The lighted tips of their cigars mingled with the sparks of fireflies and the rumble of their deep laughter and conversation. When that possibility occurred to me, I suggested to Varina that we invite Mr. Harney to visit us. My mother looked sad for a moment and said, "He's gone on, too. Maybe they're up there together, reminiscing about those wonderful days when they were young, and in the army. Your father loved that life. Perhaps he should never have left it."

Near the end of my father's life, as he and I strolled around Beauvoir and traveled together to veterans' reunions, he would occasionally talk about the rugged northwestern frontier where he had served after his graduation from the United States Military Academy. He still marveled at the horsemanship and combat skills of the red-skinned men who, he confided with self-conscious pride, had adopted him "as a brother." He never bragged of his own prowess, except to mention that he had named a horse he won races with Red Bird for one of his warrior friends.

Were they fond of him because he was their match in hair-raising exploits, or because he had married their sister in a tribal ritual—or both?

If he did marry their princess, the Indians must not have held it against him when he departed without taking his bride with him. As a farewell gift, they had presented him with an elaborate feathers-and-hide costume, which, many years later, Burton

Harrison wore in a tableau entertainment at the Executive Mansion in Richmond.

How could the man who told me never to step on an insect abandon a child he had sired? I wanted to believe he had never known of that boy's existence. Perhaps the young woman did not inform him of her pregnancy, or didn't know of it herself until after he had left the area. Then I remembered Jeff's telling me of a mission he was sent on, to rescue a white boy who had been stolen by a tribe. He had found the child in excellent condition, happy, and quite reluctant to be separated from his captors. If I could bring up the subject to him now of that long-ago desertion of his half-breed son, I believe my father would rationalize without a twinge of guilt: *Don't feel sorry for him, Winnie. The man's had a good life up there where he was born, among his mother's people.*

The only other request I've had for a lock of my hair came from Fred Wilkinson. He clipped it himself with a small pair of gold-filigreed nail scissors he took from a pocket of his waistcoat, as I was thinking that those dainty shears looked as if they belonged on a lady's vanity table, and that his hands were not as big as mine and were more delicately formed. I found that very slight touch of effeminacy endearing. Yet, the calves of his legs reminded me of the kind of men I had seen only in photographs, such as boxers in gymnasium events. I loved looking at him and touching him. I could startle him into quick arousal by sinking my tongue into the deep cleft of his chin. He reminded me of my ladies' man brother. After Varina developed a dislike for Fred and asked what it was I found so appealing about him, I told her he bore a strong resemblance to Jeff Jr. I meant in their physical appearances, although the latter had had a devil-may-care expression on his face, while Fred's was earnest and guileless. V. responded dismissively, as though Fred, like Jeffie, existed now only in the past tense, "They both depended on their looks and charm to get them by. Neither your brother nor your fiancé came anywhere near to being the man your father was."

I could not tell her then, but I might now, should the opportunity present itself again, "If my fiancé had been the kind of man my father was, he would have tried to break my spirit before I broke his."

I have wondered what Fred did with that lock of my hair. I hope his sisters didn't find it. Now, as I write, I have a vision of them—their flat, center-parted hair looking as if it had been painted on their heads—ceremoniously hurling those snippets from mine into the flames.

In one of the last conversations I had with my father, he said he knew right away—at least, after he had spent an hour with the young man from Syracuse—that Fred Wilkinson would take excellent care of me and that I should not feel any remorse or hesitation about moving to Syracuse with him. He said, "It is a man's prerogative to decide where he will live and work. You will like that part of the country; it is quite progressive."

"And, of course, you would visit us often," I said. I did not tell him or my mother or Fred that what I had reservations about was not leaving one family, but being absorbed by, and into, another.

It was clear on the few occasions I was around them that Fred's sisters regarded me as an adversary and a rival. I tried to excuse them in my heart, as I could understand their wanting to protect an older brother (who, since their father's death, had been the head of the household) from avaricious women. And I was envious of them for having brothers. Their mother was obviously concerned that I might expect too much in the way of luxury. However, I got on well with Henry, the younger son whose education Fred was providing, and I especially liked Mrs. Wilkinson's cousin, Miss Louisa May Alcott. The only time I was ever with that extraordinary writer, we had a friendly, spirited discussion about literature. When Louisa asked me if I had read Harriet Beecher Stowe's novel *Uncle Tom's Cabin*, I told her that indeed I had, and while I admired the author's verve and passion, it appeared to me that she had no firsthand knowledge of her subject matter. Fred began to fidget as I continued, "I understand there was growing concern in the North back then that the interference of Abolitionists would cause mayhem and insurrection in the South."

Louisa said, "Yes, that is true. But my dear, do you believe slavery would have ended without the efforts of those zealous and idealistic people?"

"Probably not anytime soon," I admitted. I asked her if she had read Caroline Lee Hentz's novel, *The Planter's Northern Bride*, which was published in 1854 as a rebuttal to *Uncle Tom's Cabin*. "Other books appeared around that time for the same purpose, but Mrs. Hentz's was the best of the lot. The fact that she had been reared in the North, yet lived in the South during slavery, added an element of veracity to her story."

"I am not familiar with the author, but I would like to know more about her."

I could see Louisa was genuinely interested, and not just being polite. "She was born Caroline Lee Whiting, in Lancaster, Massachusetts. On her mother's side, she was a Danforth, and on the paternal side, Caroline was descended from the Reverend Samuel Whiting, who helped settle the Massachusetts Bay Colony."

"How did this woman of such staunch Puritan stock end up in the deep South?"

"She married an itinerant, penurious, and mean-spirited schoolmaster. They lived in North Carolina, Kentucky, and Ohio, before coming to Florence, Alabama. There Caroline taught in the academy her husband established, raised crops, had four children, and helped support the family by becoming one of the South's most acclaimed ante-bellum authors. Her last book, published in 1856 shortly before her death, was a novel based on her own situation, as the wife of an unstable, extremely jealous man. But it has a happy ending, with the heroine artfully persisting until she finds her own true personhood."

"Ah," Louisa said, clapping her hands. "I am always delighted to learn about resourceful women. That this gifted and determined writer achieved recognition for her work—and while she was still alive—is encouraging to others of our gender. It is always remarkable when a woman who must attend to the needs of children and a demanding husband finds the time to give voice to her own inner muse."

After I returned to Mississippi, I sent to Louisa the two novels I had mentioned by Caroline Hentz and some examples of my own prose. Louisa had given me two pseudonymous potboilers she had written years before: *A Long Fatal Love Chase* and *Pauline's Passion and Punishment*. Reading those boldly imagined fictions on the sunlit porch at Beauvoir, I thought with a quickening of heart that this imaginative, industrious author could be my literary soul mate.

A few months later, in 1888, Louisa May Alcott died two days after visiting her father's deathbed. I could identify with her strong feeling of connection to her father and understand how she might want to join him in an afterlife, rather than stay here without him. But my main reaction to that news was selfish disappointment, that she would not become an important mainstay of my life. At the time, I was so irrational as to take her demise as an omen that Fred and I were not meant to marry.

Among the anonymous, venom-filled letters that have found their way to us was one with a Memphis postmark, addressed without prefix to Varina Davis. I opened the envelope carefully so that it could be resealed if the communication appeared to be intended for my mother. Which it did, but I would not show it to her. As soon as I read it, I burned the sheet of ripped-off tablet paper with its brief, stark message in crude block lettering (which, however, I could not forget): "How can you live with yourself, much less show your face in public, knowing that your whoremonger husband was involved in the murder of the finest leader this nation has ever known?" There was no signature and no return address.

The cruel rumor that Jefferson Davis had been at the root of Abraham Lincoln's assassination did not circulate for long; there was never a shred of evidence that Jeff was involved in that crime. As Varina explained to all who would listen, her husband had learned with a sinking heart of the untimely death of the Republican President, who, he believed, had harbored no personal malice toward him. Unlike the Republicans in Congress, Mr. Lincoln's aim was to reconcile; he would not have called for vengeance. Two days after Jeff and his cabinet evacuated Richmond, the Union President arrived in that city without fanfare, in a small boat. It was reported that Mr. Lincoln took the river shortcut from General Grant's encampment and walked uphill on Clay Street to the Confederate White House, which rose three stories high. Those who observed said the tall man admired the Executive Mansion's strong Federal facade and the oval-shaped front hall where he ascended the staircase to the second floor. There, in an office between the large nursery, where toys were still scattered about as though the children would be returning, and the bedroom where the children's parents had slept, Abe Lincoln sat in Jeff Davis's chair behind Jeff's desk. Perhaps that conflation of putting himself literally and figuratively in the place of his nemesis enabled the victor to see, in those moments, from the vanquished leader's perspective. Not that he didn't already. Years before the War began, Mr. Lincoln had expressed an empathetic view of plantation life in the South: "They are just what we would be in their situation. If slavery did not now exist amongst them, they would not introduce it. If it did now exist amongst us, we should not instantly give it up."

During the Senate race debates with Stephen A. Douglas, Mr. Lincoln said he had "no purpose to introduce political and social equality between the black and white races" and noted, "There is a physical difference between the two, which in my judgment, will probably forever forbid their living upon the footing of perfect equality." He had even suggested, to an all-black delegation, that they leave this country and go to Central America.

If the President of the Confederacy had been at his White House that day, he and the Union President might have had a heart-to-heart talk about how to mend their fences. As it was, the South would be subjected to a long, harsh period of punitive retribution. No one was more aware of that prognosis than Jefferson Davis in the days following the assassination of Abraham Lincoln.

As for the South's long-running hubris over the Confederacy, I believe Mr. Lincoln would have concurred with this 1886 Springfield, Massachusetts, *Republican* editorial: "When the end came, it was the defeat of men devoted to what was in their estimation a patriotic purpose. . . . Now they gather to commemorate the lost cause, with no desire to recall it, only to recognize it for what it was to them, to assert it to the world and go about their affairs again. That is the way we read the honors to Jefferson Davis. . . . How could we respect the Southern people if they did not believe in the thing they undertook to do, if they did not honor their leaders and their soldiers? They do well to cherish the sentiment that hallows their story."

I wish Mr. Lincoln had been alive when my father told a gathering of young Mississippians in 1889: "The past is dead; let it bury its dead. . . . Let me beseech you to lay aside all rancor, all bitter sectional feeling, and to take your places in the ranks of those who will bring about a consummation devoutly to be wished—a reunited country."

Enclosed in one poison-pen letter to my mother were clippings of cartoons from several newspapers, all depicting another rumor that circulated soon after the War ended, that Jefferson Davis had tried to escape capture by disguising himself as a woman. He was caricatured in poke bonnets and hoopskirts above captions such as "Jeff in Petticoats Tries to Give Yanks the Slip" and "Is Dat You, Mammy Jeff?" I had first heard of the humiliating defamation from Maggie. She started to cry as she got into the story, then wiped her eyes and said angrily, "He was not wearing women's clothes. Mother had thrown her raglan coat over him and draped her shawl over his bare head, because it was cold and raining."

While she related the incident, my precognitive store of images replayed the scene. The day before his capture, Varina and Jeff had come upon each other's parties quite unexpectedly in a copse of trees near Irwinville, Georgia. Jeff and his staff were on horseback; his family was traveling in an ambulance wagon. My sister sat up front with the driver and sang whenever we passed through a burned-out village. Onlookers wrote about the "pretty, happy little girl" who waved to everyone and sang so cheerfully. Maggie was putting on a show (not just for these strangers, but also for her weary, frantic mother, her jittery brothers, even me, cocooned in infantile obliviousness) and acting as though there were nothing at all to be afraid of. Varina walked part of the way, with me in her arms, to lighten the load so the vehicle's wheels would not sink down in the muddy ruts. Jeff made a fateful decision to spend that night with us in a tent under the stars.

A few weeks before, on a Friday evening, the last of March, at the Richmond depot, which had been the scene of such welcome and excitement when they arrived there almost four years earlier, Maggie had clung to her father's side and refused to leave him. I was wide awake, regarding a free-falling rain from the perch of a sturdy arm. Not my mother's—she would have been embracing her husband, whom she thought she would never see again on this earth, and trying to corral the boys. Perhaps V.'s flighty, nervous sister Margaret was in charge of me, but it's more likely I was delegated to the gingerbread firmness of the maid, Ellen, or the dependable presence of James Jones, the coachman. This uneasy group of family and servants, plus the steadfast, level-headed Burton Harrison, whom Jeff had asked to escort us, had left the Confederate capital city on the ten o'clock train. Also aboard were Varina's carriage horses, which the day after she sold them in Richmond had been bought back by friends and returned to her.

Jeff Jr. had begged to stay in Richmond and fight the enemy to the end; that request denied, he asked to ride in the car with the horses, so he could stroke their trembling flanks and calm their fears. He was told by his father to remain in the passenger car to protect his mother and sisters.

A few miles beyond Richmond, the engine failed, and the train did not move again until later the next day. The cars leaked, and the Davis contingent spent that black night on wet bedding, listening to the pounding of rain on metal and the beating of their hearts.

Jeff had instructed Varina to pack nothing other than clothing for herself and the children. They left the Executive Mansion in a barouche with a small cart attached. In the previous weeks, V. had disposed of many of her personal belongings. Her silk gowns and lace shawls were recognized among the wares in Richmond shops. Books, china, crystal, and furniture were auctioned off. The money that came from these sales was in Confederate currency, which she left in Richmond to be converted into gold. Judge Reagan would bring the gold to Charlotte, North Carolina, which Jeff had determined would be our destination. He would not allow Varina to sell the flour she had on hand at the market rate of eleven hundred dollars a barrel; instead, this staple would be earmarked for General Lee's starving armies. Jeff gave Varina a purse with what little gold he had, except for one five-dollar piece. Later, during his own exodus, he would bestow that last money he had with him on a South Carolina child who had been named for him.

He had equipped his wife with a small pistol and instructed her on how and when to use it. If reduced to the "last extremity," she should show the weapon, thereby forcing her attackers to kill her. If she thought it too dangerous to stay in this country, she was to head for the Florida coast and travel by ship to Cuba or Europe. Her husband affirmed his faith in her ability to take care of herself and their children. As the train was about to leave, Jeff bid Varina a grim farewell. He told her he did not expect to survive the destruction of Constitutional liberty.

In one of the discussions Fred and I had about the issue people of both the North and the South assumed would keep us apart, he described the States' Rights theory championed by my father as "an oxymoron, in that its proponents appeared to advocate liberty for the states that wished to continue slavery, and to be against liberty for those persons thus enslaved."

Even to my ears, my response sounded spurious. "My father, his brother Joseph Davis, General Robert E. Lee, and other leading Secessionists realized the system of human bondage that facilitated the production of cotton had to end, but they knew such a transition would require careful planning. Their intention was to equip the Africans to lead lives of independence, in which they would assume responsibility for themselves and their families, before giving them their freedom. As it was, the enslaved Africans in the Southern states were cut loose with one swoop of a pen to fend for themselves."

Fred said, "I have great admiration and respect for your father. His plantations were run as fairly as they could be under the peculiar institution, in that the Africans were supervised by overseers of their own race and infractions were dealt with by a jury of their peers. These slaves were at least secure in the knowledge that they had a home and their families would not be split up." He hesitated, then spoke as though he were making some terrible confession and could hardly bear to utter the words: "But Winnie, can you fathom what it must have been like, to know that at any time you could be bought and sold and moved from place to place against your will?"

"No, of course I can't. Slavery ended before my time on earth began." As though that fact exempted me from imagining anything so reprehensible as human beings owned by other human beings. Then, feeling obliged to defend what I found abhorrent in principle, I quickly added, "Incidents of rape and murder of white people by black men were common occurrences in the South during the War and Reconstruction. Also, for your information, my father did not have a mistress in the slave quarters behind the big house."

"That would go without saying. Your father is a gentleman."

"Yet, that type of arrangement was a common practice among so-called gentlemen. My siblings visited plantations where they played with biracial children who physically resembled the white masters." I hesitated, embarrassed to divulge my suspicions, but continued, "It's occurred to me that Uncle Joe might have crossed that line. He had practiced law in Natchez before he moved to the plantation he called Hurricane, for a tempest that almost destroyed it, with a new wife the same age as one of his two young daughters. It was well known that these girls, my first cousins, were illegitimate, as he'd not been married previously. That might explain why Uncle Joe was secretive about his past."

"Do your parents put credence in that scenario?"

"I have not brought up the subject with either of them. According to Maggie, Father made it clear years ago that Uncle Joe's private life was not a topic for discussion. Our mother fell out early on with that brother-in-law, who caused her great distress during what should have been the happiest time of her life. You might as well know what a controversial family I come from, so if you're having second thoughts—"

Fred put his hands on the sides of my face and said gravely, "Winnie, how did I ever find you? You're so very different from anyone I've ever known."

Looking back on that moment now, I realize the rapt look on his face expressed not joy, but profound sadness. He knew he had no business being involved with me.

During the time I was happily committed to the idea of spending the rest of my life with the man I loved, I began to be intellectually fascinated by the subjects of infidelity and promiscuity. In the traditional South, the art of flirtation was considered a healthy practice that provided stimulation for the brain and the heart, especially in hard times. Varina played by the rules and did not humiliate her husband by getting herself talked about in that way. During the War, she had enjoyed the deferential, considerate attention of her husband's young secretary, Burton Harrison, and the sycophantic repartee of Jeff's adviser and cabinet member Judah P. Benjamin.

In sophisticated circles, it was known that flirtation was often the first step to adultery. Yet there seemed to be an air of laissez-faire, particularly on the distaff side. A man could give his undivided attention to a partner in a casino and linger with her at the game table after the others had left without getting in trouble with his wife, and she—his wife—could flatter the ego of someone else's husband. It was permissible for a gentleman in uniform to pay social calls on women, even the married ones. In the up-and-down year of my birth, Colonel James Chesnut would send his wife a list of youthful, attractive ladies he intended to visit in Richmond, whenever he could take leave of his post and join her there.

Before, during, and after the War, Jeff exchanged affectionate letters with Mrs. Clement Clay and would go miles out of his way to visit her on his travels. He also corresponded ardently with his nephew's young widow, Mary Stamps, whose house he frequently stayed in toward the end of his life, when he visited New Orleans. I asked Maggie if our mother had ever been suspicious of Jeff's fondness for Mary, the daughter of a governor of Mississippi. "Oh, undoubtedly," my sister assured me. "But he had been so good to her family, she could not complain about his giving special attention to his own kin. It was accepted that some men, and women, too, could get away with a lot, right under their spouses' noses. The saintly General Robert E. Lee maintained a correspondence with a former sweetheart long after he and she were married to others."

There was an infamous train upper-berth scandal supposedly involving Jeff and an unnamed woman, which may have been fabricated by someone in Memphis who didn't like Varina. We had lived there in the early 1870s when Jeff was president of a life insurance company, a venture that did not work out. He had chosen the offer over one he would have preferred, as vice-chancellor of the University of the South at Sewanee, Tennessee; his decision was based on concern that the college could be affected adversely by public opinion should he accept that post.

With his dwindling resources, in addition to supporting his immediate family, he continued to provide financial assistance to other relatives, including Mary Stamps. Despite his reservations about the insurance business, Jeff would have had a nostalgic feeling for his new location. Memphis was a cotton and river town like Vicksburg, near Davis Bend, where Uncle Joe had established his homeplace Hurricane, and where Jeff had cleaned out a wilderness to build the large, plain house he named Brierfield. Later, General Grant's invading forces would occupy both plantations.

My father resided in Memphis for some months before my mother and I came to join him. Maggie had been left in London with our Aunt Margaret; the boys were placed in a boarding school in Baltimore. Although Jeff deemed it cheaper to keep us in the hotel, Varina eventually found a rental house with an acceptable address. "Court Street has a nice ring to it, doesn't it?" She put the question to me, as though, at the age of nine, I was entitled to an opinion. Watching her whip that modest place into shape, I realized that my mother, who could hold her own with most men in intellectual discourse, was equally proficient in the domestic arts. An excellent cook and seamstress, she also had a passion for gardening.

When my sister and brothers were reunited with us, I thought we were on the way to becoming a normal family, but any sense I had of security and complacency was short-lived. Gentle Willie, who had almost died of typhoid in England, succumbed to diphtheria in Memphis in 1872. The next year, Jeff resigned from the business he had never taken to as he had his former occupations as soldier, planter, and statesman. By 1875, after declining an appointment to represent Mississippi in the United States Senate and an offer to be president of a college in Texas, he had no reason to pull up stakes, so we remained in Memphis. The following year, Maggie was married in St. Lazarus's Episcopal Church, which had been established a decade earlier by resentful Southerners as a protest against insurgent Reconstructionists who attended other Episcopal churches in the city.

Our parents still traveled frequently—Varina to escape the climate or just to keep on the move, as there were always people about, she believed, who might be planning to do us harm. Jeff, too stubborn and proud to ask for official pardon and the return of his citizenship, continued to search for opportunities to replenish his depleted finances. He accepted speaking engagements at veterans' conclaves and attended agricultural fairs in Texas, Arkansas, and Missouri to promote the Mississippi Valley Association, a British firm that encouraged direct trade between New Orleans and European ports. When he was made president of that firm's American branch, he moved us to New Orleans, where the home office was. We were barely unpacked before we left that exotic city to go to London, for Jeff's new business.

It was during this trip that I was sent to the school he had selected for me, in a pretty German town with a name that sounded like a growling dog or an old man clearing his throat. The sameness of the routine made my five years in Karlsruhe pass unremarkably, for the most part, if not quickly. Besides my arrival and departure, three occasions from that time and place stand out in my memory. The first was a concert I attended with schoolmates in the palace. I had a good view of the royal family but found it frustrating that I could not approach the princess, who looked to be near my age, and pay her a compliment on her elegant pink silk gown. The next event involved the same people. All the schools had turned out to welcome the Grand Duchess back as a heroine after she had thrown herself as a shield over her father, Wilhelm I, King of Prussia and Emperor of Germany, when someone shot at their carriage. As one of the German students at our institution presented the honoree with a bouquet, an American girl beside me whispered, "Winnie, I can tell from your expression you're jealous because you aren't the one giving her the roses."

"If I were jealous, it would be of the royalty, not of somebody who must bow to them." I didn't explain that the thing to be envious of was not the woman's exalted position, but her selfless courage. The Grand Duchess Luise had proven herself able and willing to make the supreme sacrifice for her father. I made a silent vow to do the same for mine, if the opportunity ever presented itself. It never did; but I have a recurring dream of lying in a pool of blood with people staring down at me. One of whom is my father, asking, with stern displeasure, why had I taken a bullet meant for him?

The third event, which occurred about midway of my time at the Friedlander Institute, was by far the most significant—but I am not yet ready to commit that one to this journal.

Margaret Connelly

SEPTEMBER 15, 1898
Having been in domestic service since I was fifteen—over half
my lifetime—I could tell tales that would raise an eyebrow or
cause a gasp, but I don't have the urge to prattle about people I
have worked for and come to know as well as I do my own family. Most of them, including my current mistress, Mrs. Jefferson
Davis, have been kind and considerate. So I say at the outset, in
the event this rumination is ever read by anyone else, that I am
writing in this diary for one purpose only—so that I might revisit
these observations when and if I have acquired the wisdom of
advanced age, should I be so lucky.

Mrs. Davis and her daughter Winnie had only been in New
York City for about three years when I started to work for them,
but their crisp way of speaking sounded as if they'd never lived
anywhere else. When I felt at ease enough with Winnie to mention that fact, she explained that her mother had grown up in
Mississippi, attended a school in Pennsylvania, and also had lived
in Washington, D.C. And she herself had spent a good part of
her life outside the South. She said, "Neither of us is of a regional
mind-set, although there are those who expect us to be." I didn't

catch the drift then of what she meant, but the words have stayed with me. One of the things I admire most about Winnie Davis is that she doesn't talk down to me. I call her Miss, but in my thoughts, I call her Winnie, the name she goes by.

Having just said Winnie's mother is kind and considerate, I will add that Mrs. Davis is a mixture of haughty and down-to-earth. Some of the time, it's as if she's reminding herself and me that we have to observe the difference in our stations. When Winnie is away on a trip or in one of her moods where she won't talk to her mother, or as she has been these past weeks, really low-sick, Mrs. Davis gets all friendly with me.

I was not supposed to be here. She had explained that she couldn't afford to bring me on vacation with them and had lined up summer employment for me in the city. Then as I was about to end that service and go to Boston to see my family, Mrs. Davis called for me to come to Narragansett Pier to help with her ailing daughter. She could have engaged hotel maids who would like to pick up extra wages during their off time, but she wanted me because I am used to the "routine." I expected Winnie to be in one of her moods where she takes to her room and doesn't leave it for days. At such times, she's not that much of a care; mainly, she wants to be left alone. This time, though, I could see right off it was more than one of her dark spells. Soon after I arrived, I overheard Mrs. Davis tell Mrs. Pulitzer that Winnie was sicker than anybody she'd ever seen not to be dying.

Mrs. Pulitzer got a city doctor involved that same day, but even he has not been able to turn things around. Mrs. Davis sent me to the village pharmacy yesterday for Dulcet's Tonic, which was the only thing she could think of that hadn't been tried on Winnie. It's hard on her to watch her daughter fade in and out, as though reality is a room with doors, so Mrs. Davis has had me doing most of the watching. At first, I was uneasy sitting by the bedside with Winnie lying there like she'd already passed on or staring toward the ceiling as though she saw things there that weren't. Winnie usually has a notebook handy, which she writes in when she feels like propping up. Not when her mother's around, though. When she hears a tap on the door, she stashes the binder under the bed-covers. She has instructed me to place it beneath her bed, should she doze off with it in her hands.

After I had coaxed some coddled whites-of-egg and soggy toast down her this morning, she rallied a bit and stared at me like she'd never seen me before. Then with a smile of surprise, she said, "You're his first wife, aren't you?"

That gave me a turn. "Oh, Miss, you know I'm not any kind of wife." I could have added, "Like you, I did not marry when I had the chance." Also like her, I'm upwards of my thirtieth birthday, and while I don't expect my status to change, if she could just stay healthy for awhile, hers might. In the city, men come to call for Miss Winnie Davis, to take her to dinner and the theatre, or to the opera, or a reception. When she puts her mind to it, she can get herself up quite splendidly and even hold her own with Mrs. Pulitzer. Right now, though, she looks pitiful, like she's in a trance. Her eyelids are half-closed—in the white space that's visible, the pupils dart around like bugs—and her breathing is shallow. That crinkly hair going every which way around her face and shoulders makes her look as bewitched as she sounds. (After writing that sentence, I have crossed myself and said a silent prayer.)

A few days ago, she rallied considerably. Winnie is more re-served than her mother, but she's not shy. She told me once she and I were both listeners by nature. "Margaret, I believe you like to form your own opinions," she said. "And so do I. Do you sometimes think you can see both sides of an argument?"

"Both, or neither. I tend not to take a side in a controversy. I guess I'm what you would call a fence-sitter."

"That can be the same as seeing both sides," she said. "It's easier to observe life than to participate in it."

Yet she had told me of times when she spoke out so forcefully on subjects she didn't know about firsthand—such as the War that was mostly fought in the South—that she even surprised herself. After such a moment, she added, "I am not comfortable in a group where everyone thinks alike."

"But isn't that the way it is down South?" I asked.

"Only on certain subjects." She frowned, then sighed. "Such as, the way things used to be, before the War."

Since she's not especially talkative by nature, I was surprised when she started to ramble that morning. It might have been the fever that got her going. First thing she said was, "I didn't know until I was almost grown that my father had been married to someone before my mother." She stared at me. "You bear a strong resemblance to the portrait of the first wife. Did you know her?"

"No, I don't believe I ever met her. Where is this portrait, Miss?"

"I assume it's still at our house near Biloxi, in Mississippi."

Mrs. Davis once told me that was the most aggravating place she could think of—hot as Hades, with mosquitoes almost the size of hummingbirds—and she didn't miss it one bit.

Winnie added, as if I had asked the identity of that first wife, "Her name was Sarah Knox Taylor. Knox, as he called her, died of malaria three months after they were married. Jeff had fallen ill too, but he survived. Knox was buried in a graveyard on his sister's plantation in Louisiana, where he had taken her to meet some of his family." She paused to cough and sip from the glass of water I handed her. "When my mother visited those same relatives on her honeymoon, she took flowers to the first wife's grave. My sister said that years after Knox died, our father ran across a pair of her slippers in a trunk and went berserk with grief."

"That's a drawback of marriage," I said. "Most always one of the pair dies before the other."

"Well put. Now, please remind me who you are?"

"Margaret Connelly."

"Of course. I must have mislaid your name." She wasn't teasing me; she appeared too dazed to be making a joke. She shook her head as if to clear it. "Days and nights and weeks have run together. Do you know when I returned from Atlanta?"

"I wasn't here then, but I believe it's been about six weeks."

"That long! Have I been out?"

I was trying to frame an answer that wouldn't alarm her. "Well, I wouldn't say you were really out of your head . . ."

She laughed for the first time since I've been here. "I meant outside this hotel."

"No, Miss; I don't believe you've left these rooms."

"Then let's take a stroll." She sat up and swung her long legs over the side of the bed and stood up.

"Your mother—"

"She's not here, is she?"

"No, ma'am."

She pushed her hair back with an angry gesture. "Good. It's not up to her anyway."

She walked fairly steadily to the armoire, flung the doors open, took a shirtwaist dress off the rack with one hand and started to pull her chemise over her head with the other. She can be fit to faint one minute and have a burst of energy the next.

Winnie Davis was standing there naked as the day she was born, unfastening the buttons on the dress.

"I'll do that for you, Miss. But first, let's get you some undergarments," I said.

"No petticoats or stockings. In the summertime, the less clothes the better."

I didn't have the heart to tell her summer is gone and we're well into September. After I got her into the clothes, she let me brush her hair and coil it into a loose bun. She did not look at her reflection in the glass. I held out a hand mirror to her, and she shook her head. "No, thank you. It would be like seeing my own corpse," she said.

"Miss, if I may say so, you look amazingly well." That was not flattery. She still has a fine shape, curves in the right places, even though she regurgitates most of what little nourishment she takes in. At that moment, her complexion had a becoming glow and her large eyes that remind me of silver coins were so luminous I wondered if the fever had stoked some fire inside her. Winnie was eager to be off, but I took time to write a note, informing Mrs. Davis that we were taking a bit of air, and left it on the console in the foyer.

We had just got off the lift in the lobby when I spotted that lady holding forth in a group near the front entrance. "Shouldn't we speak to your mother?"

"No. We'll slip through a side door."

Outside, she took several deep breaths and stared longingly toward the water. Then her gaze lit on the bicycle stand. "Margaret, can you ride a wheel?"

"Yes, Miss."

"Excellent." She took a small snap purse from a pocket, extracted some coins, and handed them to me. "That should get us a pair of bicycles." I was glad she didn't specify a two-seater, as I'd had no experience with that kind of contraption.

We rode at a sedate speed, side by side on the boardwalk beside the seawall, not briskly, as I suspect she would have preferred had she been feeling up to par. The breeze was tender on my face, and I thought the tingling, salt-misted air must be good for her.

Although her mother gives me my orders, Winnie is the one I am a wee bit leery of, even when she's well. At times, she seems distracted and acts as if she's unaware of my presence, but not in a snobbish way. At the apartment in the city, she spends hours at a time writing at her desk, and two or three times a week she goes to the newspaper office. She and her mother are not like other ladies of the leisure society. These two work for wages. The older likes for the younger to dress well, but her own clothes are much-mended. When I first spoke with her, I figured the famous Mrs. Jefferson Davis would haggle about salary, but I also got the impression, during that interview, that she was a fair-minded person. Some from the South who've come North to live will have only colored servants, but Mrs. Davis explained, when I came to apply for the position, that she likes to hire a good Irish Catholic girl. Even though she herself is a lifelong Episcopalian, she's a great admirer of the mother-church religion and doesn't mind if some of it rubs off on her. I wanted to suggest she start coming to Catholic services and get it firsthand, but of course, I said no such thing.

There were no people about when Winnie and I ventured outside the hotel; most of the summer residents had departed by the end of August. After a few minutes of riding and listening to the rattles and squeaks of chains and pedals, I pretended I was winded and needed a rest. When we had plopped the bicycles down on the ground and ourselves on an iron bench beneath a tree, she asked me if I had a serious beau.

"Not at present, ma'am. The only man who ever proposed to me has gone his own way, and although it has been five years since we left off keeping company, I still think about him sometimes."

"I know that feeling." She hugged herself then, not as if she was cold, but as though she was pretending her arms were someone else's.

"Are you sorry, Miss, that you didn't marry the man you were engaged to?" I would not have been more surprised if worms had come out of my mouth. I could scarcely believe my nerve.

Neither the impertinence nor the question seemed to faze her. Looking out at the sea as though she saw something there, she said, "I don't argue with fate. Marriage between us was not in the stars." Then she turned toward me and added brightly, "Dear Margaret, if you had been meant to marry that fellow, you would have; so don't make yourself miserable about it."

I've never had a minute of misery over ending things with Will Jackson, who had more love for drink than for me. My motive in telling Winnie about him was to get her talking about her own broken engagement, which I was curious about because a few days before, when we got together in the village on our afternoon off, Mrs. Pulitzer's maid had told me what she claimed was the real story: The ghost of Winnie's father, the Rebel president Jefferson Davis, had appeared to Mrs. Davis and ordered her to cancel the wedding plans, as he could not bear the thought of his daughter marrying a Yankee. Mrs. Davis did not dare disobey her husband, especially since he was speaking from the other side, so she did as he instructed. If I was going to find out anything more on the subject, this was the time, so I took a deep breath and asked boldly, "Has the man you were engaged to wed someone else?"

The question seemed to surprise Winnie, as if she'd not even considered that possibility. After a moment, she said, "If he had married, or become engaged, or was seeing someone seriously, I would know."

"Yes, there are some people who will always see to it that we hear things we don't necessarily want to," I said.

She said, "I meant, I would know in my heart if he had fallen in love with someone else."

I wanted to say, "Then you must still be in love with him," but the closest I got to it was, "It seems a shame you didn't get together then."

"Yes, it does, doesn't it? Yet at the time it seemed impossible." She sighed and frowned. "He had financial problems that could not be resolved in the foreseeable future." She sounded as if she was quoting something she'd read, or memorized. After a few seconds, she continued. "I hoped to earn money through my writing, but I wasn't sure I could, and I didn't want him and his family to regard me as a liability. Also, I won't deny it, I was not happy at the prospect of living with his widowed mother and three sisters."

I didn't know it happened in the upper registers of society—
that a new wife would have to move in with other members of the
man's family. "Well, Miss, maybe we are both better off," I said.

She was staring at the water again, as if she might wade into it
and keep going until she disappeared beneath that ink-colored
surface. The stone building with the life-saving station was not far
away, but I was relieved when she accepted my suggestion that we
start back, and that we push the bicycles, instead of pedaling.

When we reached the suite, Mrs. Davis had not returned. I
retrieved the note I'd left for her and put it in my pocket. Winnie
said, "Thank you for accompanying me, Margaret. Please don't
mention the outing to my mother."

"I won't, ma'am." After I helped her change back into the chemise, she lay on the bed with her hands by her sides and closed
her eyes. Within seconds, she looked so out of this world I implored her silently to hold on and not give up.

SEPTEMBER 17, 1898

One of the doctors was here most of the morning, pacing by the
windows and tapping a wooden tongue depressor against his palm.
With each thud of that little paddle, he would wince as though it
hurt. Mrs. Davis rolled her eyes toward me, as if to say, "That fool."
After he left, she went to her own room to rest, so there were just
the two of us in this one, the sick girl and me. All of a sudden,
the thick fog outside the windows lifted, and sunlight streamed
in like good tidings. In these recent sad days, I had learned to be
with Winnie in the silence, and I had the feeling she appreciated
my company, even when she appeared not to be conscious. Mrs.
Davis's older daughter, who lives in Colorado, has been wanting to

come, but Mrs. Davis has put her off, telling her to wait until Winnie feels more herself and they can have sisterly companionship.

Mrs. Pulitzer and her retinue have left Narragansett Pier, but she has stayed in close touch. Mrs. Davis stood by Winnie's bed this morning and read aloud the latest wire from that lady: "I am coming back, angel; arrive tomorrow. All my love, Kate." Then she said brightly, "And won't we be delighted to see her. If anyone can pull you out of the doldrums, it would be Kate."

Winnie gave no sign that she took in a word of that.

The quiet around here is almost scary. All the other boarders and most of the staff have gone. The owners of the hotel have allowed us to stay on after the summer season ended because Winnie is too sick to be moved. A priest from the Episcopal church in the village has been stopping by each afternoon to read to her from a prayer book. Yesterday, when he tried to give her Holy Communion, he could not get her to open her mouth enough for the wafer, and the wine dribbled down her chin.

It was also yesterday that something very peculiar happened, either to me or to her, or to both of us. I was sitting right there, on the chair a few feet from the corner of the bed, watching Winnie intently, as I was supposed to, when a silver cloud rose from her body and moved to the ceiling. At the same time, I heard her breathing stop with a wispy sigh, as if she knew what was happening and didn't mind. "Oh, good-bye, dear Miss," I whispered. "You must be in heaven now, or on your way there."

She opened her eyes and said, her voice clear as a bell, "No, I'm not. I'm thirsty. May I have some water?" She seemed to be pretty alert that afternoon. Her mother had come in to sit with Winnie; I was in the kitchen when a basket of fruit was delivered to the apartment. I took the basket in to them, and Mrs. Davis read the foreign-sounding name on the card to Winnie, with the greeting: "My dearest Winnie, please send for me the moment you feel like having company." Mrs. Davis said, "I told you he really liked you. You should write to him, and show some interest."

Winnie pulled the sheet over her head.

SEPTEMBER 18, 1898

This morning, Winnie's eyes seemed brighter, and she seemed less listless. The local doctor came by and was pleased to find her temperature was down to almost normal. "We're making progress," he said jovially to Mrs. Davis as he left to have coffee with Mr. and Mrs. Burns. Mrs. Davis had hardly slept the night before, and needed to be alone, so she retreated to her room. "I declare, Margaret," she said, just before she went through the doorway, "I don't believe I've ever known anyone as quiet as you. I think you must emanate a peacefulness that Winnie admires, and that's why she likes having you in here with her."

As Winnie began to stir around, I went to get her a small dish of cut-up fruit I'd prepared from the basket sent by the man Mrs. Davis wanted her to show some interest in. I had begun to think the way that lady talked: "Soon, we'll be able to take our girl back to New York. Then she'll perk up, because she'll be anxious to get back to her writing. She'll also want to check with the publisher about her novel, go to the newspaper office, and see some friends again. . . ." As I set the dish on the dresser, the mirror's reflection was eerie. The person on the bed, who seemed to be asleep, was more than asleep. There was not the slightest evidence of movement—no flutter of an eyelid, no breath parting her lips, no twitch of a finger. She was as still as a wax figure. She looked like pictures I'd seen of enshrined saints in European cathedrals. It was straight-up twelve o'clock noon. The clock on the bedside table marked that fact with a weak chime, like a little bird singing its last notes. And this time, I knew my mind was not playing a trick. I told myself: *This has nothing to do with me.*

And yet it did. I reacted as if someone were giving me instructions: touched her lips with my rosary, made the sign of the cross on her forehead, adjusted her gown so her breasts were not exposed, straightened and folded the counterpane below her crossed hands. Then I sat beside her on that bed, cradled her beautiful head in my arms, and silently, wordlessly, made my farewells to Winnie Davis. As soon as I was able to control the flow of my tears—I had not let myself sob audibly—I felt beneath the bed ruffle until my hand grasped the notebook I'd seen her put there the week before. I took it to the alcove where I slept and put it with my things in a cupboard. Then I did what I had dreaded the most, and had known ever since I came to Narragansett Pier that it would fall to me to do; I went to Mrs. Davis's room to give her this dreaded news.

I rapped softly on the door. As soon as she opened it—I had not yet said a word—the woman let out a scream that would do credit to a banshee, then put her back against the wall and slid slowly down it. The bulk of her made a loud thump, like a sack of meal hitting the floor. I hurried to the foyer and pulled the bell cord. A man on the hotel staff responded promptly, but seeing the situation, decided to wait outside the door for Mr. Burns to arrive and take charge.

Mrs. Davis was still sitting on the floor with a stunned look on her face as I slipped away to the alcove, to kneel by my daybed and say a proper prayer for the soul of Varina Anne Davis, whom the world knows as Winnie, the Daughter of the Confederacy.

Winnie's Notebook

MAY 29, 1898

On this day in 1881—seventeen years and half my life ago—I left boarding school. My mother, who has never hesitated to request favors of friends and friends of friends, had asked Miss Emily Mason, who lived in Paris and would be traveling in Germany at that time, to collect me in Karlsruhe and take me to the glorious City of Light, where I would live under her wing until they came to get me. I could hardly sleep the night before; the departure I had looked forward to ever since I arrived at the Friedlander Institute was finally about to happen—unless there was some last-minute complication, such as the elderly spinster I was to be released to having a change of plan or heart. Varina's letter had described this chaperon as "quite sprightly for her sixty-odd years." I took that to mean Miss Mason was only slightly bent over and got around reasonably well with a cane.

I was waiting anxiously on the front gallery with my trunk, portmanteau, and hatbox when she arrived at precisely the time her note had specified. To my surprise, V.'s description was not euphemistic: Miss Mason was indeed sprightly, and also caneless. She walked with long strides and with purpose, as though each

step she took was important. She smiled at my self-conscious curt-
sy and told me to call her Emily. Her gloved hand tilted my face.
"The picture your mother sent was of an adolescent girl. But you,
my dear, are on the verge of becoming an extraordinarily attractive young woman." For the first time, I realized the term *woman*
has more dimension and possibility than the pallid noun *lady*.

While Emily supervised her driver's stashing of my luggage, I
scrutinized her angular profile and smoothly coiffed, iron-gray
hair and noted the smartness of her slim-skirted, pin-striped suit
and the crisp white blouse that resembled a man's shirt. The
headmistresses loomed like Valkyries in the doorway. I knew
they were glad to be seeing the last of me. The other new gradu-
ates had departed the day before, after the awarding of certifi-
cates. (The one I received had my name wrong—*Verrine Anna
Davies*—but the error would not be discovered until my mother
unfurled the scrolled document months later, in Mississippi. At
first she was furious, then she laughed so heartily I heard a seam
rip.)

As the cab clattered down the cobbled drive, I had no desire
to look back at the dreary, gargoyled stone mansion that seemed
out of place in that hospitable, fan-shaped city of neoclassical
architecture and beautifully laid out parks. Emily had instructed
the driver to take us to the railway station, where we would board
a carriage train for Paris.

I was aware that my companion was a highly regarded scholar,
the former headmistress of an elite school, and the author of
several books. In our first conversation, which was timid on my
part and enthusiastic on hers, I learned that she had lived in
Paris for years but intended to move back to the United States
eventually. And she has done so. At present, Emily divides her

time between her country house in Maryland and an apartment in Georgetown.

After sharing a compartment in a train that looked like its miniature counterpart in Black Forest shops, we arrived the next morning in the city that five years before my father had deemed too morally decadent to entrust with a young girl whose parents would not be close by. Probably by dint of her having involved Emily, Varina had got him to agree to my having this sojourn in Paris.

By the time we were settled into a cab with a French-speaking driver, my companion had made it clear she would not be an overly attentive chaperone. She casually outlined how I would spend the weeks before my parents would arrive to take me off her hands: "I've signed you up with Antoine Duval, who directs an art school, which is conveniently located a few blocks from my apartment building. I suggest you take a studio class and a lecture series. Also within strolling distance is a small conservatory, should you desire to further your musical vocation, as your mother suggested; and a dear friend of mine has offered to tutor you, at his house, in the French language and literature. You may decide how much time and energy you will expend on these pursuits, Winnie. Be sure to save some time to educate yourself with visits to the Louvre." She smiled widely, as a boy would. "Now that business is out of the way, and you're still a captive audience, I have a need to speak of the famous old times in our native land." Not for herself, as she implied, but for me: She must have sensed how I needed to have gaps filled in.

Like my father, Emily was a native of Kentucky; her father had been the first Secretary of the Michigan Territory. She had become acquainted with Jeff in Detroit, when her brother was Governor of Michigan. "This was just after the Black Hawk War. Your father was in charge of a detachment to escort the defeated but proud chieftain, Black Hawk, through the country. Jeff would not permit bystanders to gawk at the prisoner when the riverboat made stops. During that excursion, he allowed some of Black Hawk's braves who had cholera to be put ashore, as they requested, so that their spirits might travel together to the sacred hunting grounds. Jeff was amazingly poised for such a young man—he carried himself straight as an arrow, and he was quite handsome." She had next encountered him in Washington. "While serving in President Pierce's Cabinet, your father earned the reputation of being one of the country's best Secretaries of War. I heard his eloquent farewell speech to the Senate after Mississippi elected to secede from the Union. And of course, I saw your parents frequently in Richmond, during the War." Emily shook her head as if to clear a vision. I would come to recognize that gesture in others when they simultaneously referred to that city and that time. "We next encountered each other in Paris. Jeff was greeted with much affection by the large contingent of Confederates who had moved abroad—among them, John Slidell, formerly of Louisiana, whose daughters had married Frenchmen, and across the Channel was his old friend Dudley Mann, who adored your father. Dudley offered to set Jeff up in the horse business in England. . . . You've probably heard all this many times before."

"No, I've not heard very much from him or my mother about those times. I have been aware of my father's fondness for Indian lore—He would sing their songs and tell me their myths—but I have never heard him mention the Black Hawk incident." Having gathered my nerve, I implored her, "Please tell me all that happened to him after the War ended. Most of what I know about my earliest years came from my sister. Maggie described how we had to flee Richmond, when the Union troops were moving in on that city, and about the family's clinging to each other and crying when the soldiers took Father off the ship. But I didn't know where he went. It's been five years since I've seen my sister. The letters Maggie wrote to me in Karlsruhe seemed forcibly light, as though she was determined not to reveal anything that could upset me while I was so far away."

Emily said, "That was a kindness. Your sister had been sent away to school also, so she knew what you were going through, missing your family." She reached out and touched my cheek gently. "As for what happened to your father after he left the ship, you must understand, it is not my place to discuss that subject with you. However, I shall tell Jeff when I see him in a few weeks that, in my opinion, you are mature enough now to hear him talk about it."

I did not have to remind her. Soon after my parents arrived in Paris in late August, Emily spoke privately with my father, then repeated his response to me verbatim: "The past is unalterable. I don't wish the girl to grieve on my account, and I cannot risk prejudicing her against the United States. I want Winnie to love her country."

My disappointment must have shown, as Emily continued calmly: "The President of the Confederacy was imprisoned for two years at Fortress Monroe. He was never brought to trial and was finally released. Your father may never bring himself to discuss that humiliating experience with you, but you should know that your remarkable mother lightened his load then—indeed, she may have saved his life—by persisting until she obtained permission to move into that compound with him. And of course she brought you with her, and your presence provided the only delightful moments he had there."

I managed to smile. "Thank you, Emily. You've relieved my mind tremendously. I had been taunted by a girl at school who said my father had been thrown in jail and left to rot and just missed being hanged. But Fortress Monroe has a dignified sound, as though it's not a real prison—"

"It seemed very real to him. With the addition of iron bars and concrete, a gun casemate had been turned into a cell. The fort was encircled by a moat over a hundred feet wide," Emily said. "However, when I visited your father there, I noted he could glimpse Chesapeake Bay through the bars. I did not see you that day; I believe you were sleeping. I was told the guards were entranced by the prisoner's little daughter, who would compliantly dance a jig for them whenever they asked." She must have heard that from Varina. Jeff would never have made such a lighthearted remark about that most onerous period in his life.

I could not then and still can't visualize that silly little girl who whirled like a dervish, trying desperately to entertain men who had shackled her father in leg irons.

Prior to that conversation, I wondered if Emily had been enamored of Jeff, because she spoke of him more often, and with more affection, than she did my mother. But even before I observed her around him, I knew that romantic infatuation had not entered into their relationship. The men she invited to her literary salons appeared to admire her unconditionally, but it was evident to me and no doubt to them that, for Emily, emotional attachment to the opposite sex had never been part of the equation. This remarkable, independent woman has been a role model for me in many ways, with one significant exception: I cannot imagine how it would be never to have thrilled to the touch of a man.

During the summer Emily generously shared with me, we resided in an ivy-encrusted building near the Right Bank. Traditionally, the Southern expatriates who left after the War (and some during it) flocked to that area of Paris. She had secured a two-room pension on the fourth and top story for me; her apartment was on the second. I liked the idea of having my own space, but I worried that my parents could not afford for me to have this luxury. V. would have taken it for granted that I would be Emily's houseguest and not be charged for my lodging. When I was at school, the dismal fact that my parents were constantly strapped for funds seeped through the ink of their correspondence to me. On several occasions when my tuition and board were past due, the Misses Friedlander had deprived me of milk and dessert until the tardy payment was received. As Emily unlocked the door to what would be my quarters, I asked her if my father had made provision for the rent. She had already told me he'd sent a sum to be parceled out to me for spending money.

"There is no charge for the apartment. My friend who has the lease is spending the season in Venice. She'll be happy her rooms are being occupied." She drew the skimpy curtains apart and cranked open the casement windows. "There. When you feel lonely, the city will keep you company."

As if responding to a command, stale air scurried out like an animal, and in wafted a scent of recently rained-on foliage and fragments of a language in which I was not yet proficient. That first night in Paris, I hardly noticed the rank odors of refuse and garbage that floated up from the street below. I was filled with nostalgia for someplace I could not name, where the warm, heavy air was intoxicatingly sweet, and white, tan, brown, and black people all spoke softly, stretching vowels into diphthongs and slurring consonants, so that words conveyed meaning even if they sounded unintelligible.

Although I was anxious to see my parents, I was also eager to make the most of this unexpected interim of independence. I quickly adjusted to the routine. In the mornings, I walked five blocks along the banquette to the art school; in the afternoons, in the opposite direction, I cut through a park (where lovers entwined, as though choreographed, on benches and on the ground beneath trees and behind shrubs) to Monsieur Elliard's cottage, which smelled of cinnamon and garlic, for two hours of instruction in the French language. The first session dealt with vocabulary and speech, the second with literature. At the end of the week, kindly, white-haired Monsieur brought in small cups of chocolate and allowed me to choose a book from his overflowing shelves to take with me, for practicing the art of translation. I selected Maupassant's new novel *Une Vie* (*A Woman's Life*) and became so immersed in that saga of a frustrated wife it was as if I had created the character and determined her fate.

Emily approved of my decision not to take singing or piano lessons. "Germany is excellent for music. Here, there are many other areas to occupy your attention before you return to your country."

My country. I could not imagine myself ever saying the phrase. I had never thought in that context before.

Frequently, Emily and I dined at the Café Guerbois with her friends and acquaintances. The group included several brusque, opinionated females who spoke English as fluently as their own language. The first time, after I was introduced, one of them said to Emily with a wink, "What a pretty bauble you have there."

Emily replied, "Winnie is not an adornment. She is the daughter of the most brilliant man I have ever known and a gifted person in her own right."

My instruction had not officially begun, but I was already learning. *Pretty* can be a meretricious, demeaning adjective, and women who do not need men in their lives can be just as spiteful as those who do.

During that hiatus in Paris, I made one significant friendship on my own. Claudia Leveque, from New Orleans, was in my art appreciation class. She was sixteen, a year younger than I. At midday, we would sit together in the school's courtyard and share whatever was in our luncheon boxes. Mine contained simple enough fare: Each morning, I purchased a roll, a piece of fruit or a cluster of grapes, and a small wedge of cheese at a market on the way to the school. Claudia would bring beignets, pâté, pralines, jellied chicken or boiled sausages, all prepared by her mother, whom she referred to as Mama, with the French pronunciation. "Mama has nothing else to do here but cook and sew. She does not like to wander about on her own, because she is afraid of being accosted by men," Claudia explained. "I tease her: 'Mama, do you really think you are that irresistible?'" The two of them had come to Paris for Claudia to acquire, as she put it, a smattering of culture.

I told Emily I would like to invite my friend to tea. "Claudia is from New Orleans, but speaks the French language as though she's lived here all her life. She's the most beautiful girl I've ever seen. Her hair is the color of midnight sky and very glossy."

"Ah." Emily busied herself opening an envelope as she asked, "Is your friend a Creole of color?"

"I don't know." I wasn't familiar with the term, but the implication was clear. "Her skin is not dark. In Memphis, I used to reach that shade of brown from playing outside in the summer months. Claudia's mother is here with her."

"I look forward to meeting your friend. Ask her for Thursday afternoon, and of course, include her mother in the invitation."

I followed Emily's instructions, but Claudia came alone, noting vaguely that her mother was indisposed. When Emily remarked that her fine posture suggested she might be a dancer, my friend replied, "I had lessons in ballet until I turned thirteen. Then the ballet mistress said I had grown too tall." She confided to Emily what she already had to me, "I would like to be trained in the cancan while I'm in Paris, but my mother and our patron would have fits if I so much as mentioned that idea."

"And your patron is . . . ?"

"Mr. Roger Fontaine, of New Orleans."

Emily smiled brightly and stirred her tea. "I see."

And despite my naïveté, so did I. I had begun to wonder if the man Claudia spoke of often to me—at first as "Mr. Fontaine" and then as "Roger" and always with excitement in her voice—had initiated her into the rites of physical love. I never would have asked her, but a week or so later, she informed me. "I have not been alone with him. However, there is an understanding. When Mama and I return to New Orleans, we will move into a commodious *maison* on Rampart Street, and Roger can stay overnight with me there whenever he wishes."

"What about your father?"

"He lives with his wife and their children."

At the time, Claudia was peeling an apple with a tiny silver knife. As she answered my question, the knife slipped and nicked her finger. The wound was slight; she wrapped the handkerchief I handed her around it and said, "That was a reminder I am not supposed to think about them. But now that I've started to tell you, I shall finish. Winnie, I have two half-brothers I have never met. The day before I turned ten years old, I told my mother all I wanted for that birthday was to see Papa, who had not been coming around for some time. The next morning, a Sunday, my mother took me to watch my father and the lady he had married several years before and their two young sons emerge from a large Protestant church in the Garden District. We remained inside the carriage, peeping through drawn curtains, so they would not spot us. From that distance, they looked like a dollhouse family: perfectly formed, and white. Mama said, 'Now that you have seen these people, forget about them. Whenever they come to mind, dismiss them and wish them well. Otherwise, you will bring misery on yourself.'" Claudia tucked her head and appeared to be intent on smoothing wrinkles out of her skirt. I recognized the diversion as one I used when overcome with emotion or a shame I did not understand. Just as I was about to put my arms around her to comfort her, Claudia lifted her chin and said, "I have not seen my father or his family since that day. Although he does not maintain contact with us, he has made provision for our welfare. My mother bears him no ill will; therefore, neither do I."

"When will you marry Mr. Fontaine?"

The question seemed to irritate her. "I don't know. But I shall have a good life. Roger is kind and generous and he loves me."

A few days later, when I arrived at the lecture class, Claudia said casually, "I did not bring a lunch today. Mama has instructed me to bring you to dine with us in our suite. Then we'll send you off in a cab, so you won't be late for your French tutorial."

Of course, I accepted. The small lobby of their hotel exuded an air of jewel-toned elegance, despite the tawdriness of grime-encrusted window ledges and threadbare carpets and draperies. When I met Claudia's mother (who insisted I call her by her first name), I understood why she had declined to come to tea at Emily's. Elaine Leveque, a handsome woman, was considerably darker-skinned than her daughter. Cheerfully friendly without meeting my glance or taking my hand, she immediately occupied herself with the mechanics of getting us fed. She poured wine into glasses and ladled a thick, steaming concoction of fish and vegetables into large, almost flat bowls from an ironstone tureen that had the name of the hotel imprinted on its lid. She urged second helpings on us in an almost scolding voice (while I tried not to show my mouth was on fire from the finely minced peppers) as she replenished the bread-and-butter plates. When she explained the technique of getting sugar to caramelize on the crème brûlée, it sounded as if she were reciting poetry. Later, when Emily asked me what we talked about, I could not think of anything the hostess had said directly to me other than to ask where my home was. I had replied, "Memphis, Tennessee, is where we lived before I went to Germany. My parents now reside on the Mississippi coast, near Biloxi."

"Not far from New Orleans, then," Elaine had said, and frowned.

Claudia immediately chimed in with, "Isn't that wonderful, Mama? Winnie and I can be friends forever."

As Claudia accompanied me to the street floor that day (I had declined the offer of a cab; I have always liked a brisk walk, especially after a rich meal), she explained what I had not asked: "Both my mother and I were fathered by white men. One of Mama's maternal grandparents was half-white, which puts her between mulatto and quadroon. And I am very nearly full-octoroon." At the time, I was not familiar enough with racial terminology to realize being seven-eighths white was the ultimate level—any more dilution and a person would not have to add that qualifying phrase *person of color* beside his or her name.

"Your mama is quite vivacious," I said. I had noted their resemblance to each other, although Elaine Leveque's nose was wider and her lips were fuller than Claudia's. The woman's proud, almost angry demeanor proclaimed her awareness of who she was and how she came to be that person.

"Thank you for seeing that in her," Claudia said, as though she were responding to my thought rather than the spoken compliment. She added, after a moment, "A child of mine could have light-colored eyes and fair skin that turns golden in the summer—like you, Winnie. If her hair is amber and gently curls like yours, she will not be compelled to press it straight with a hot iron. And she can pass."

"Pass?"

"For white."

"Would you want your child to pass for white?"

She stared at me. "*Mon Dieu!* How long did you say you've been away from that country?"

"Five years."

"That's not long enough to forget what it's like there. If you really don't have any idea why I would want a child of mine to pass for white, I suggest you ask your parents or Miss Mason to explain." As though deliberately masking her natural grace of movement, Claudia stalked ahead of me, kicking small stones off the sidewalk.

I watched this flaunting of temperament with a mixture of exasperation and appreciation. I thought, *If I were Berthe Morisot, I would want to paint this girl, who is the pale beige color of Parisian buildings and of milk that has been enhanced with a few spoonfuls of coffee, right now, in the exquisite, near-sepia light of early afternoon.* I had spotted the artist twice that summer—once at the Louvre, when she appeared to be studying Correggio's work, and the other time in a park, executing a plein air scene with such concentration she seemed oblivious of everything else. (This remarkable woman, who died a few years ago, was my favorite among the Impressionists. I admired her perseverance in a field dominated by men, and for being known by her maiden name, although she was married to Édouard Manet's brother.)

As I was contemplating my vision of a self-assured artist rendering immortal her impression of my beautiful friend, the latter said exuberantly, "Winnie, don't you wish we could stay here forever? Paris is a soufflé of a city. New Orleans is a mysterious gumbo, like Mama's soup; strange things lurk below the surface. You can be surprised at what turns up on your spoon." Claudia added in an exaggerated drawl, as though parodying someone, "Yes, ma'am—have to watch yo'self in N'Waleans." Shards of sunshine sliced through the density of leaves and branches, depositing copper glints in her hair. She put an arm around my waist and pressed her firm cheek to mine. She smelled earthy and sweet, like the gardenia shrubs my mother planted around the house we rented in Memphis. "Darling Winnie," Claudia whispered.

Flustered, I said what I was thinking: "Your face reminds me of the way a peach feels."

"Really? Then from now on, whenever you bite into that luscious fruit, you will think of me and send me good wishes."

I asked her seriously, although she may have thought I was being flippant, "Are you invoking some aspect of Voodoo?" I knew little about the superstitious practice, other than it was prevalent in New Orleans.

"Heavens no. Roger has forbidden me to have anything to do with what he calls 'that silly mumbo jumbo.'"

"How can he forbid you?" I almost added, *Since he's not your father and not yet your husband.*

"His terms are reasonable. He doesn't want my curiosity about the supernatural to lure me into trouble. Although my mother insists that Voodoo is primarily a healing art—she claims that Marie Laveau, a devout Catholic, had permission to hold rituals behind the St. Louis Cathedral—I have no desire to dabble in it. And I hope Roger doesn't suspect, as I do, that Mama had a conjure woman put a spell on him."

"Why would she do that?"

"To make him fall in love with me."

"Have you asked her if she did?"

"No, because I would rather believe this romance with Roger is my divine destiny and not contrived through magic. Roger has also instructed me not to frequent Congo Square, where I learned, as a child, to dance without constraint, as the spirit moves me." A wide, secretive smile transformed her face. "Of course, he will like seeing me dance that way, if it's just for him."

"But he should not deprive you of visiting a place that's part of your heritage."

Claudia was weaving her heavy mantle of hair, which the wind never seemed to disturb, into a loose chignon. "It's of no real consequence, since he has agreed that we will live in the old French Quarter—Vieux Carre—from which I can be aware of the rhythm of the drums."

I persisted, "Are you going to let Roger dictate what you can and cannot do?"

"I have no choice in the matter. Isn't it the same for real wives?"

"Not always. My mother, who has a fierce streak of independence, has been known to defy my father's wishes." The last time I had seen V., she had come from London to my school in Germany to tell me she was going back to the United States. "But not to that awful woman's house in Mississippi," she'd said. "I shall never spend a single night under Sarah Dorsey's roof."

Claudia said, "So, when your mother refuses to do his bidding, does your father beat her?"

"He would never raise a hand to her. But he lets her know of his displeasure." He punishes her with verbal rebuke, silence, and hardest of all on her, his absence.

"If your mother wants to be independent, why did she marry?"

"She was very much in love with him."

"It sounds as if your mama is one of those hysterical women who thrive on making life complicated. I don't want turmoil. I yearn for peaceful companionship with a man who will protect me." She shivered, involuntarily. "I just felt a cat walk over my grave. Are you familiar with that expression?"

I guessed its meaning. "A foreboding that something unpleasant is about to occur?"

"More than unpleasant. Sinister."

"My nurse, Mary Ahearn, believed turning around three times could dispel a bad omen."

"Really? Was Mary Ahearn your black mammy?"

"No, she's fair-skinned and Irish-American. She's retired now, but I stay in touch with her."

"She can't be both Irish and American," Claudia scoffed. "She has to choose which she will be called."

"No, she doesn't. Mary was born in Ireland and she lives in America."

"Then should people who were born in Africa, but live in America, call themselves African-Americans?"

"I don't see why not."

"Winnie, you are even more naive than I thought. Why would anyone, especially me, want to label herself as African?"

"I never implied that you would or should."

As we approached the corner where we would part, the brushing of our skirts against each other seemed to stir up friction between us. Claudia had not spoken in several minutes. "Are you irritated with me?" I asked.

"No, I am not thinking about you at all. I am praying. When I attended the convent school of the Ursuline nuns in New Orleans, I imagined myself joining their order when I grew up."

I almost laughed. Then I decided she was serious. Her hands were pressed together in prayerful alignment, and her lips moved silently.

That night, Emily attempted to explain Claudia's situation to me. "In New Orleans, the elite system of concubinage known as *placage* does not carry the stigma of prostitution. It's feasible, even likely from what you've told me of your friend's mother, that she would insist Mr. Fontaine sign a contract with specific guaranties, such as his continued financial support of her daughter in the event he should decide to end the relationship."

I could not imagine Claudia's being abandoned by a man she'd given herself to heart and soul. I said firmly, "I'm sure he will marry her."

"Dear, don't get your hopes up there. Although it occurred occasionally during the chaos of Reconstruction, biracial marriage is illegal in New Orleans."

"Claudia has said the house will be in her name. And Mr. Fontaine will provide for their children's education, and they would inherit from his estate."

Emily nodded her approval. Her smoothly coiffed gray hair reminded me of a barrister's wig. She said, "It used to be a tradition that the *placee*'s children were assigned scraggly lots in town, and the man's legitimate offspring would inherit the sugar cane plantation. Then after the War, those small parcels of property on Canal Street became more valuable than the homestead acreage on the bend of the river. Apparently, from what you've told me, Claudia is pleased and optimistic about the arrangement her mother and Mr. Fontaine have made, which is probably as good as it can be under the circumstances. Be happy for your friend, Winnie, and wish her well."

Three days before my parents were due to arrive in Paris, Claudia's mother took her away. I wondered if Elaine Leveque pushed up their departure schedule to avoid any possibility of encounter with the man who had been the leader of the Confederacy. I assumed she would have stronger feelings on that subject than Claudia, who had informed me their ancestors who came to New Orleans from Saint Domingue and Cuba were not slaves, but *gens de couleur libre*. She had introduced the topic offhandedly, although her voice revealed her pride: "My great-grandfather, whose name on the register was followed by 'f.m.c.,' which stands for 'free man of color,' was a prosperous silversmith. His daughter Agatha married a French Creole, Phillipe Guillot, in the Church. Despite being ostracized by the gentleman's family and most of his white friends, Agatha and Phillipe stayed together, and now they lie, one above the other, in a mausoleum in the Saint Louis Cemetery."

I had the feeling then that Claudia knew whose daughter I am. Hoping to offset any preconceived image she might have of Jefferson Davis as the enemy of black people, I said, "Robert Brown, a man who was a slave before I came into the world and who insisted on remaining with our family after he was emancipated by the Proclamation, has been like a grandfather to me."

"But that former slave is not your grandfather," Claudia said. "None of his blood flows in your veins."

I tried again. "When we were living in Richmond, a baseless rumor went around that my mother was part Indian. And my mother's response was, if that statement were true, she would not owe anyone an apology. Toward the end of our time in that city, she rescued a young mulatto child from a bad situation and brought him home to live with us."

"In the servants' quarters, you mean?"

"No, he slept in a room with my brothers. He was called Jim Limber. My father had made application in the courts to adopt him, but at the War's end, Jim was taken away. My parents tried to discover his whereabouts, but could not."

Claudia sighed with exaggeration, as she often did before making a point, and said, "That boy is old enough now to get in touch with your family on his own. If he hasn't he must have figured those white people really didn't care much about him one way or the other."

At that moment, with her lips pursed unbecomingly, she reminded me of girls at school. When I first arrived at the Friedlander Institute, a student from Charleston had whispered behind my back, "Winnie Davis has delusions of grandeur. She believes her father was King of the South. But he wasn't king of anything, and now he's nothing but a pauper. The Davises have to depend on the charity of their friends."

Claudia asked—and I detected a note of compassion in her voice—"Do you ever dream about that little darky who was almost your brother?"

"No. All that happened before I was two years old." Jim was a photograph on Varina's shrine shelf: a small brown boy in a velvet jacket and breeches, standing on a chair looking sad and solemn, as though he knew his time in that household was running out.

Claudia had met Roger Fontaine on her sixteenth birthday at a Bal de Cordon Bleu. I didn't know how that structured system worked until after I returned to the United States and became a frequent visitor to New Orleans. From a book I found in my father's library at Beauvoir, I learned that the custom began late in the last century, when drums would beat on street corners to send the signal that a ball for "colored ladies and white gentlemen" would be held on a certain night at the Salle de Condé. In addition to the gentlemen, those early events attracted an undesirable element of the white male population, so the price of admission was raised enough to make the balls unaffordable for men who "smelled bad and would start fights." By 1815, quadroon balls were held in all the public hotel ballrooms in New Orleans and became as much an institution as Mardi Gras. To qualify for the selection process, a girl could not be more than one-quarter Negro (preferably less) and should be well-mannered, poised, and intelligent. The only men of color allowed to attend the balls were the musicians who played in the dance bands.

Justin Charles, a not overly serious suitor who was one of my escorts during my coming-out season, bragged that he had attended blue-ribbon balls with a friend who was seeking "an amorous liaison of that sort," which, however, he himself "most certainly wasn't."

I said, "But you must have entertained the idea."

"Truthfully, I did not. On each occasion, I was empathetically embarrassed for those beautiful, demure creatures who were put on display by their mothers to be haggled over as though they were prize fillies." Just when I was thinking Justin had more character than I'd given him credit for, he added, "Besides, if my father thought I was involved with a gal who'd been touched by the tarbrush, he would flat out disown me."

Henri Goulard, a vain young instructor who seized any opportunity to speak English, gave me the news of the Leveques' departure from Paris. I had just taken a seat in his lecture class and placed my luncheon box on an adjacent chair to save it for Claudia. Henri (he insisted I call him by his first name) leaned over me and said softly, "I have been informed that your—chum? Is that the word?—has withdrawn from the school and will not be returning." He pulled a gaudy fob watch out of a vest pocket and pretended to consult it. "At this moment, Mademoiselle Leveque and her mother are likely boarding the ship that will take them to *Nouvelle-Orleans*, in the United States of America." He could tell from my expression (which must have been a pastiche of shock, hurt, disbelief) that I was more than merely surprised, but he continued relentlessly, "I realize you have tender feelings for her. Such crushes are part of growing up. But you and Claudia are meant for the opposite sex, and would have parted soon, in any case. Win-nee, you must learn to be more discerning. That girl is not on your level. You are gifted in sketching and painting, but she? Not in the slightest! And she is not capable of the subtle aesthetics of art comprehension. Of course, Claudia has an abundance of personal charm—that spontaneous laugh, and the way her derrière bounces as she walks—"

"Did you hope to seduce her?" I heard those words as though someone else spoke them and wondered which was worse, my audacity or his.

"What a delicious question! *Oui*, absolutely, of course!" Henri stroked his face with one hand, which made me think of my father, trying to stroke away the pain of neuralgia. My father would be appalled at this arrogant dandyisme who chattered on, ridiculously, "I should have approached her early on, after she first arrived. I do believe she had an eye for me. Did she ever mention me to you?"

Only to make fun of your efforts to get her attention. "Not in that way. Claudia is engaged to be married."

"Ah, well, it's water over the reservoir then. But there's still time for you and me to become more deeply acquainted—perhaps you can dine with me this evening? Can you slip away from your guardian to meet me?"

"Probably, but I would not wish to, since I, too, am in an arrangement."

"And what would that be?"

"I am promised to a gentleman who owns half the state of Texas."

Henri laughed as though the fabrication were more preposterous than I intended it to be. "You Americans are so heartless, always joking about serious matters." As he turned toward the lectern, his hand grazed my breast. I pretended not to notice.

I did not let his boorishness keep me from the few remaining class sessions. I was interested in his topic, "Jacques-Louis David and the Neo-Classicist Style of Painting," and I was determined to get Emily's money's worth for this enrichment. However, from then on, I made sure to be among the last to arrive and the first out the door of the arrogant Frenchman's class. There was no further conversation between Henri Goulard and me until I was about to leave after his final lecture. Assuming he had just included me in the perfunctory best-wishes-and-good-bye speech to students he did not expect to see again, I was startled when he pulled me aside as I was about to pass through the doorway. Keeping his hand firmly on my arm and addressing me by a name he knew was not mine, he said, "Winifred, I shall miss you and that tempting Negress friend of yours. I wish I could show both of you, together, what Paris is really all about."

"You're fortunate my hands are full of books," I said. "Otherwise, I would slap your face."

Later, after I saw that Monsieur Goulard had given me the lowest mark I ever received in a course of study, I wished I had informed him that in America, unless they are professional actors, men do not wax their mustaches and eyelashes. The report card was of no consequence, as my parents considered my academic education over and done with when I finished school in Karlsruhe. They had arranged for me to have the summer in Paris for the same reason Claudia's mother had brought her there. We were gems in the rough, to be polished for acquisition. Claudia, of course, had already been marketed. In my case, the honing was speculative, with loftier aim. I was not to be some man's discardable mistress, but his lifetime appendage.

Claudia had said her birthplace was "a charmed and blessed city, favored by the angels as well as by the spirits of Voodoo."

My father would have agreed with her that the city was blessed. He had deemed it a miracle that New Orleans, which was commandeered by the Union Army early in the War—in April 1862—did not suffer massive destruction in that conflict as other Southern cities and towns did. New Orleans's population had been assimilated from several nationalities, each with its own caste structure. A blend of French, Spanish, Acadian, African, and English—spoken, shouted, and sung in a variety of accents—floated over courtyard walls and levees. I found it strange that the embankments that kept the river from inundating the city were called levees, the same word my mother used in referring to daytime social receptions.

Soon after I returned to this country and became acclimated to life at Beauvoir, my parents and I took a steamer from Biloxi to New Orleans on a Friday, to pass the weekend at the St. Charles Hotel, where they had spent their honeymoon. The next day, while Varina shopped at the French Market, Jeff took me on an educational horse-car excursion. Actually, the tour was a repetition of one he had taken me on shortly before we embarked for Europe; but on the earlier occasion, I had sat on his lap and almost drifted off to sleep enjoying the comforting drone of his voice. This time, I took the seat by a window of the trolley and paid attention to what he was saying.

"Canal Street is the widest business-district street in the country—over 170 feet across. This area, which New Orleanians refer to as 'neutral ground,' began as a commons between the original city, the Vieux Carre—which extends from downtown to Esplanade and from Rampart to the river—and the newer American Quarter upriver. An artificial waterway was to be constructed in the middle of the thoroughfare to connect the river to the Basin, which connects to Lake Pontchartrain. However, the plans did not materialize, so Canal Street is named for something that was never built."

The area he referred to was a parklike preserve of grass and trees, in the center of which parallel rows of track framed narrow beds of pebbles, so the horses and mules that pulled the cars would not slip in wet weather. On the sides of this commons were roadways paved with large stone blocks, which had crossed the

Atlantic on ships, as ballast. "Perhaps the route is lovelier without a waterway," I said, remembering the sight and smells of floating debris on the Seine.

An attractive, middle-aged woman in a plumed bonnet was sitting across the aisle. Although she appeared to be reading a magazine, it was clear to me that she wanted to speak to my father. As though prompted by an offstage director, she leaned toward him and said, "Mr. Davis, the residents of New Orleans hope you will decide to make your home here."

Jeff replied noncommittally—he was a great admirer of New Orleans and enjoyed visiting there—then snapped open his folded newspaper and used it as a shield. The woman flushed slightly over the dismissal and gave me a speculative glance. I could read her thought: *Is that young woman his latest romance?*

Ever since I learned she had left Paris, I had assumed Claudia and I would reconnect in New Orleans. By the time I got my bearings there and could navigate the city on my own, I had lost my nerve about seeking out the Leveques. I had mentioned my new friend in letters from Paris to my parents, but her name had not come up since I was reunited with them. Jeff would be so dazzled by Claudia, he might miss the clue that her skin was a shade too caramel. Varina would see immediately that Claudia was delightful and bright and good-hearted—everything she would want in a close companion for me—but would the shrewd, practical Mrs. Jefferson Davis risk alienating the prominent families of New Orleans by allowing her daughter to associate socially with someone of mixed race, if such were not an acceptable practice?

I had no idea what the protocol was, and Emily Mason was not around to advise me. Since I could not bear the thought of

Claudia's being snubbed on my account, I decided not to try to find her. If she happened to turn up somewhere at the same time I did, we would rush to each other with arms outstretched, and she would give that whooping laugh: "Win-nee! *Mon Dieu!* Is it really you?" Yes, that was how it should happen—naturally, uncontrived, and without awkwardness. A chance encounter on a busy boulevard, in a restaurant or streetcar, or at the bustling market on the corner of Rue Decatur and Esplanade Avenue would be a sign that Claudia and I were meant to resume our bond of friendship, and everything would work out fine.

Before I went away to school, I had learned from my father that most of the urban area streets were on a parallel bend with the river or in spokelike right angles to its curve, which is how New Orleans came to be called the Crescent City. Now that I had accepted the probability (there were no premonitions) that one day I would be numbered among the population of this complex metropolis, I set out to find out more about it from my parents, books, and articles, and also from new acquaintances who took for granted their birthright privileges as multigenerational New Orleanians. Soon I began to feel as though I had been born and reared there too. One of my favorite spots is Jackson Square, in the Vieux Carre. Originally called Plaza d'Armas or Place d'Armes and utilized as a military parade and execution ground, the section was renamed almost half a century ago to honor General Andrew Jackson, who saved the city in the Battle of New Orleans in the War of 1812. The magnificent bronze statue of this hero on horseback has him waving a tricornered hat in triumph. "Or perhaps," my father added slyly, "he's tipping his hat to the Baroness Pontalba, who might be looking through one of those lace-curtained windows across the way."

The story of Micaela Almonester de Pontalba fascinated me. On land she had inherited from her father, the Frenchwoman had constructed, in fine European style with shops on the ground floor, the first apartment buildings in this country. The initials of her maiden and married names are woven into the design of the iron railings on the balconies. The Baroness supposedly supervised the design and the construction and fired any architect or workman who did not do exactly as she wished. Legend also has it that only a few years before, in France, while trying to divorce her husband, she had been shot four times by her father-in-law—but the Baroness Pontalba survived, won her divorce in the French courts, and got back the money her husband and his father had stolen from her.

After New Orleans was founded in 1718 to enforce the French claim to the Mississippi Valley, French colonists arrived by the thousands. Their settlements extended to all the nearby bayous. Next to arrive were Acadians who had been expelled from the lower east coast of Canada. The city was passed back and forth between France and Spain for most of that century. When colonial trade restrictions were lifted, steamboats flocked like ducks to the Mississippi River, bringing goods from the eastern seaboard and Europe. The sudden spurt of prosperity also brought an influx of Americans from the Northeast to an area dominated by proud descendants of Europeans who had settled Louisiana. Although ruled for forty years by Spain, New Orleans received its cultural temperament, as well as its name, from the French component. The aristocratic Creoles, who were used to controlling the commerce and civic affairs, branded *les Américains*, who caused the population to double in the 1830s and '40s, as unwelcome opportunists. It didn't matter whether they were bankers, architects, engineers, and entrepreneurs who would contribute substance, style, and structure to the existing mores or grubby sorts like gamblers and pirates—all were disdained. For the next fifty years, the old and new factions vied with each other for supremacy. Realizing they were not wanted in the Vieux Carre, the Americans began an expansion uptown, purchasing, subdividing, and developing the plantations along the crescent of the river. One of the new sections, Faubourg St. Mary, soon competed with the French Quarter as the main business district.

Concurrently, the port city had taken a prominent role in the slave trade and become a haven for free persons of color. After the War, with the immediate formation of the Reconstruction government, universal suffrage, marriage between races, and equal civil and political rights for all citizens were legalized. A decade later, when the siege officially ended, Federal mandates that had protected black people during that postwar era gave way to a new Louisiana State Constitution, which retracted citizenship rights so recently granted to the ex-slave population. Also affected by this reform were the freeborn people of color, who were reduced to a status lower than what they had before the War. And still to come—in 1890, almost nine years after Claudia Leveque and I parted in Paris—the enactment of Louisiana Legislative Code 111, spurred by a group of prominent Creoles, would define all persons of African ancestry as "legally and in fact *Negro*," thereby stifling any claim Creoles of color might harbor to being eligible, by virtue of their mixed ancestry, for privileged treatment under the law.

Before that time, however, I had learned enough of Claudia's story to know that she would not be affected by this edict.

On the way to the initial meeting of debutantes and their mothers, Varina gave me a tutorial. "Since you've become acclimated to living in the South again, you appear to be quite comfortable around our friends, but standoffish among your contemporaries. Winnie, you must realize that, in this kind of society, being accepted by your peers is of vital importance." Tiny beads of moisture, which must have been due to nervousness since the weather was still cool, collected on her forehead and upper lip as she continued. "As the outsider coming into the group, you will have to befriend these girls on their terms. You must act as though you're interested in whatever they have to say, but do not inject a serious topic into what may seem frivolous conversation. And please, Winnie, remember not to lapse into German."

"Would French be permissible?"

"Well, yes—most of these families are of French extraction— but don't be the one to initiate it."

My question had been intended as mild sarcasm. Normally, V. would enjoy such banter, but now she was deadly serious. "In this initial phase of your association with young women who have known each other since they were born, you will be judged on the way you express and present yourself. On the other hand, do not worry, as any anxiety will be reflected on your face."

I was curious as to how long the trial period would last before I was granted or denied the approval of this peer group, but not enough to ask Varina. She squeezed my hand, I supposed to give me courage, as the driver brought the carriage to a stop in front of an imposing residence on Prytania Street, at the head of the Garden District. I wished I had come there with easel, canvas, and paint box, to attempt an Impressionist-style rendering of the double-galleried house in its verdant setting of trees, vines, and shrubs. As we walked up the brick-paved pathway to the entrance gallery, Varina whispered the names of plants she recognized— Confederate jasmine, tea olive, bougainvillea, pomegranate, plumbago, rice paper, palmetto, elephant ear—as though reciting a mantra. I was thinking both of us would be more at ease among this placid vegetation than we would be inside that houseful of women. Also, more pleasantly, I was reminded of Berthe Morisot's painting of her sister holding a butterfly net and the sister's family taking their leisure in a *jardin* such as this one.

After the greetings and introductions, the mothers congregated in a parlor that resembled an antiques emporium, and their daughters were directed to another, which was furnished sparingly and charmingly with wicker chairs and settees. Those in the latter group stared at me, exchanged knowing glances, and stared at me again. Irene, the most self-assured of these girls and obviously the leader, twisted her rope of pearls and said, as though her mind were really elsewhere, "Winnie, I understand you were at a boarding school in Germany for several years. Did you feel completely lost in that strange country?"

I wanted to say, "Yes." Instead, I said, "Only until I learned to speak the language."

"And how long did that take?"

"By the end of the first month, I could fend for myself."

"Heavens. Imagine learning that difficult tongue in a month!" She stuck our her tongue and rolled it suggestively. Two of the others giggled, as though she'd made a joke at my expense. Irene said, "Well, Mama says your parents are brilliant people, so it's logical you are quite brainy yourself. Did you have a sweetheart over there?"

"No."

"No?" Irene said, as in exaggerated disbelief. She took a sugared strawberry from a silver bowl and daintily devoured it in three bites, then dropped the stem end into a waste dish, before returning her attention to me. "But you're quite pretty. I should think you would have sparked considerable interest from the boys' academy."

"There wasn't a boys' academy. The only option for romance was to cuddle with girls, and I didn't fancy any of them."

The spontaneous remark elicited a wave of melodious laughter. Irene composed herself first and held her hands out to quiet the others. "Winnie, none of us has been so far away from home for as long a period as you have. We insist that you share some of your unique experience with us."

Assuming she meant something titillating, I was about to improvise on the Sapphic theme when I heard myself say, in the slightly guttural accent my mother had been trying to rid me of, "The only boy who befriended me in Germany looked as if he had been created by Michelangelo. His name was Hans, and he worked in the school's dairy." Then the flow of memory banked as quickly as it had begun—an intuitive warning that I should not share my introduction to Eros with these girls who watched me as though snakes might crawl out of my mouth.

Earlier in this notebook, I decided to postpone getting into that subject. Now, for whatever reason—the impetus may be the way this particular pen fits my hand, as though it has become part of me—I am ready to record my impressions of that milestone event.

The first time I was aware of Hans, I felt a connectedness with him and wondered if we might be distantly related. He looked at me with a depth of affection I had never come across outside the realm of family. I was fifteen; he was a year older. Our names and ages and his avowal of passion for me were the sum of our verbal exchange on the only occasion we were together. After strolling past the school's barn every Tuesday for several weeks with a nature-walk group, I realized this beautiful, fair-haired boy always came out of the building just as we approached, and that his attention, like a capricious sunbeam, would dance lightly over the group of girls, then focus on me. That day, I returned his gaze so intensely he blushed. The following Tuesday, he was standing diffidently aside as the line of girls came by in single file, some with handkerchiefs clamped over their noses to deflect the stench from the barn. As I drew level with him, a scrap of paper moved as though of its own accord from his hand to mine. I furtively read what he had written in a childish scrawl in his language (he did not know a word of mine): "Lovely girl, please to come home with me Thursday. Is my day off. I meet you at back gate at two o'clock. My mother will make us tea." With a furtive nod, and without breaking pace, I accepted the invitation. After we turned onto a side path, a girl behind me tapped my shoulder. "The stable hand could get in trouble for staring at you, Winnie. He must have heard the silly rumor about you."

"What would that be?"

"That you're royalty."

"What makes you think I'm not?" I turned my back to her, but I wanted to butt my head into her. Maggie said I used to do that as a small child so often other children would refuse to come to play with me.

At the appointed time two days later, I waited for Hans at the gate in the wall that bounded the school property. There was not anyone in the immediate vicinity to notice as this boy and I tacitly, silently, our arms touching like hot logs in a fireplace, made our way along a jagged path through weeds that rustled like cornstalks. The pace he set was too fast for conversation. I was slightly behind him when we arrived at a small house, which looked as though it belonged on a cobbled street instead of at the edge of an uncultivated field. His mother opened the door, bowed as though she were a servant, and said not a word. She placed a plate of cakes and two cups of dark, steaming tea on a table beside the straight-backed chair where, she indicated with a gesture, I was to sit. Then she scurried away and I heard an outside door creak open and shut.

The woman had left her son and me alone, except for a caged finch, in the tiny, steep-roofed house that smelled of turnips cooked sometime in the past (or countless times: the aroma had a ghostly quality). Neither of us ate a crumb of those cakes. As Hans knelt beside the chair and kissed and fondled me with what seemed reverential adoration, the little bird made excited noises with his wings but did not chirp. During Hans's ministrations to my body (which he concentrated on as though doing lessons for a master), I could see, through a narrow-paned window, his mother toiling doggedly on her knees in a stony patch of ground, and I thought longingly of my own mother, who at that moment might be strolling along a garden path in her floppy straw hat,

humming and talking to roses and gardenia blossoms as she severed them from their bushes and dropped them into her basket.
When Hans walked me slowly back across the field to the school,
he kept a damp, glowing arm tight around my waist and repeat-
edly kissed my mouth and neck. Then, through the cloth of my
dress (which when I put it on had been pridefully stiff with starch
and now was limp, as though in shock), he pressed his face into
the hollow between my embarrassed, upstart breasts. As we approached the gate between that field and the school's property,
he put his open mouth on mine for the last time and groaned as
though he knew it would be just that: the last time. I returned to
the dormitory in a daze and was glad I did not have a roommate
for that term, so I could be alone with my feelings. I threw myself
across the cot and imagined Hans thinking of me in the same
way I was thinking of him, and I wondered when we would be
together again.

At the sound of the supper bell, I hastily rubbed flesh-colored
chalk from my paint box onto the flower-shaped bruises on my
face and neck. On the way to the dining hall, I was intercepted by
a smirking girl who said I was to report immediately to the office.
There, the Misses Friedlander took turns chastising me about my
regrettable behavior. I had left the premises without permission
and in the company of a hired peasant, with whom I engaged in
wanton caresses, in full view of passersby! If I signed a prepared
statement of apology, which included a promise never to have
another rendezvous with Hans Bruehoff (that was how I learned
his last name), they would not report the shocking and shameful
incident to my parents.

Hans was ordered never to set foot on the premises again. I
gleaned that information in harsh fragments from his mother

two days later, after I sneaked out of a chapel service and ran all the way to their house. I did not have to use the door knocker; the woman was waiting in the doorway. She began to screech at me with such agitation it was difficult to translate what she was saying. When she raised an arm as if to strike me, I fled and did not look back until I had almost reached the gate. Then it was Hans who was standing in the doorway of the house, but I could not tell from that distance whether he was smiling or weeping. I remained in Karlsruhe for two and a half more years, during which time I never had a glimpse of him, or a message from him, or any news of him.

I came out of my brief reverie when Irene said, in a languid voice, "Well? Don't keep us in suspense, Winnie. Did you have a torrid love affair with Hans?"

I wanted to tell her an impertinent question does not require an answer, but I remembered Varina's admonition—I was to make friends of these girls, not antagonize them. So I told a truth: "We spent one afternoon together, which resulted in his banishment and a big tongue-lashing for me, from the headmistresses. I did not care about myself, but I felt badly about his losing his livelihood because of me. However, I was able to put the episode behind me by concentrating on other things." By other things, I meant my studies, but Irene took it differently. Her face lit up and her auburn curls bobbed with what even Varina would have agreed was approval. "So, you could rise above the incident and your crush on Hans in short order, because you knew there would be other fish to fry. Welcome to our inner circle, Winnie Davis. You are proud, passionate, and a risk-taker, yet you are also hard-nosed and practical. All of which makes you one of us." She gave me a sisterly, jasmine-scented kiss on the cheek. The other girls fluttered around us like exotic moths.

During that year's Mardi Gras revelry, these young women individually and collectively projected a starlike force of privileged innocence and sophisticated élan. They knew how to sip champagne over a course of several hours without becoming tipsy and how to look deeply into a man's eyes without seeming brazen. I could imagine my friend Claudia in this company. They would admire her guileless bravado, even as they secretly denigrated her for thinking she could ever be completely de-Negroed. That first afternoon, I asked my new inner-circle friend, when we were not within earshot of the others, "Are you acquainted with Roger Fontaine?"

"I know who he is. Why?" Irene shrugged as if the subject were boring.

I shrugged to shake off the feeling I was about to indulge in gossip. "Two years ago, in Paris, someone told me he is a very attractive, worldly man."

"Winnie, you would not want to become involved with Roger Fontaine. He's too old for you, and he would not be considered a proper escort. He is known to frequent houses of prostitution, and he makes no secret of it."

"Where are these houses?"

"The most well known are in the Vieux Carre."

On the way back to the hotel, I asked Varina what a house of prostitution was.

She said wearily, as though it pained her to talk, "Oh, Winnie. I am not surprised to learn that you picked up that sort of terminology in Paris. But it is not a topic for young ladies to discuss in polite society." She closed her eyes, shuddered to emphasize how distasteful the subject was to her, and did not answer my question.

The next day, after the pleasant ferry ride back to Biloxi and a dusty buggy ride to Beauvoir, I immediately went to my room to look up the word *prostitution* in my dictionary. It wasn't until I had absorbed the more fulsome account in Jeff's heavy, gold-tooled encyclopedia that I thought, *What an amazing and ingenuous way for women to earn their livelihoods.*

SEPTEMBER 12

When I am lucid, as now, my memory is on fire. I have re-read what I've written here, and it makes sense. I try to edit my work objectively, and I realize that in this story of my life—which now appears to be fiction, since it is all in the past—I must tie up a dangling cord about my friend Claudia.

It had been five years since the Leveques left Paris. She—not Claudia, her mother—recognized me before I did her. "Miss Davis?"

"Yes? Oh, my heavens, is that you, Elaine?" I hugged her, and I felt her tense up, then relax into the embrace. I quickly looked around, expecting her daughter to be in the vicinity.

The woman said so softly I barely caught the words, "Claudia is no longer with us, except in spirit."

At first, I thought she was implying archly that Claudia had run away. Then I read the real meaning in her sorrowful eyes. "Oh, no. Oh, my dear Elaine." We were standing beside an outside table of a café near the entrance of Lafayette Park. I put an arm around her waist and said, "Can we sit down here, or should we go somewhere else?"

"Here is fine. I am fine. I can tell you everything now without wailing or making a scene."

A waiter was hovering. "Shall we have coffee, or tea?" I said. "Are you hungry?"

"No. But yes to coffee." After it arrived, she poured the steaming liquid inside each of two cups, then did the same with the warmed contents of the cream pitcher, and stirred sugar into hers before she enlightened me further. "Claudia was happy. She loved the house Roger had provided for us. At first, he would come there for dinner, and stay for awhile. Then, after a few weeks, he began spending one night a week there, then two nights, then three. Claudia knew I missed my own cottage and neighborhood, and she insisted I move back there. She said, 'Roger and I are like a married couple now; we do not require a chaperone.'" Elaine paused and took a few sips of her coffee.

I did not prompt, nor did I try to imagine what she was going to tell me. It occurred to me then that I had been carrying on conversations with Claudia in my imagination whenever I had occasion to visit her city.

As Elaine resumed, her voice hardened. "Roger Fontaine was not as much in love with Claudia as she chose to think. He was enchanted by her youth and beauty and her elegant manners, but he had no intention of having a family with her. He had expected me to enlighten my daughter about contraception, and I had done so. That is, I had tried my best to make her aware of what was available."

I nodded. I could not murmur politely, "I understand," although I thought I did: Claudia had wanted the ultimate respectability. She thought the quickest way to get Roger to marry her would be to become pregnant with his child. I said, carefully, "I seem to recall Claudia's having said that children born of their union would inherit from him."

"I did manage to get that concession from Roger, but during the bargaining, he made it very clear to me that he did not want children, at least not anytime soon. Winnie, I had told Claudia not to tell you, but while we were in Paris, I took her to a special class where a highly respected French courtesan demonstrated the various devices, methods, and techniques that thwart conception yet enable a man to have his pleasure."

"She did not tell me," I said truthfully. My thoughts were now in turmoil: I was shocked and saddened about my friend, anxious to know how she had died, yet also curious as to how she had reacted to that class taught by the French courtesan.

"When we returned to New Orleans, I reminded Claudia that she must initiate a frank discussion of her new knowledge with Roger and let him choose the method of contraception they would use. She said she did not care to discuss the subject with me and asked that I not bring it up again. You may not have been aware that Claudia, by nature, was very modest."

"Yes, I believe I sensed that about her," I said, although I had not.

Her mother continued, "She was uncomfortable when I tried to give her practical advice about how to make love to a man and how to please him, in the hope that she would become indispensable to him. She wanted romance clothed in mystery, not details and instructions—but it was my duty to see that she understood the rules, and the responsibility that rested on her. What could I have done differently? I ask myself that question every day."

"I'm sure you did everything you possibly could, under the circumstances," I said mechanically.

"Within a few months after the liaison began, she became pregnant. Roger was not at all pleased. He told Claudia she must have the pregnancy terminated."

Elaine twisted a spoon in her hands. I wondered if she wished it were Roger's neck. She said, so softly I had to lean forward to hear, "Although I was seeing my daughter almost every day, I was kept completely in the dark. Claudia did not tell me she was expecting, and I failed to see the signs. Neither did she inform me that she had told Roger the news. Apparently, she had thought he would be as happy as she was. It must have crushed her to realize that was not the case; Roger told me later she had assured him the matter had been taken care of. He assumed I had made the arrangements and been with her during the procedure. That's what he called it—'the procedure.' But she had done nothing about her situation, other than to lie to him. Then one night when he was away on a business trip, she began to hemorrhage, and a servant came for me. The first I knew of my child's being with child was when she began to miscarry. We took Claudia to the hospital, but she had bled too much. In her delirium, she asked me if the baby was a female. What had come out of her was a bloody mass, but I told her yes, I believed it was a girl. Claudia said, 'She is to be baptized Winnie Davis Leveque. If she lives and I don't, I want her to be brought up by the nuns. And if I live, and she doesn't, I will become a nun.'"

In the bustling ambience of that public square, Claudia's mother and I sat with our faces in our hands and sobbed together. Tears fell like rain into the snowy-white napkins on our laps. Then, wiping her eyes and recomposing herself with a fierce, grave majesty, Elaine said, "Enough of this sad business. Let's talk about you, Winnie. Are you in love, or have you been?"

"Alas, I am not, and have not been."

"Well, you will be, and soon," Elaine predicted. "Take my word for it: I know these things. You are ripening, and glowing; you're a peach, waiting to be plucked. And now, you must come with me to my house. Claudia told me that you love to learn; she said you were the most conscientious student she'd ever known. So I am going to instruct you in a way you likely have not been educated before. I will teach you how to take care of yourself, Winnie Davis. Tall, slender girls like you and Claudia are not ideally suited for having babies. And even though you may decide you want ten children, you shouldn't have to become pregnant until you're ready."

I accompanied Elaine Leveque to her house and paid close attention to all that she showed me and told me. A few weeks later, I met Fred, and fell in love as swiftly as one might fall down a flight of stairs. Although I disregarded Elaine's first cardinal rule—"Don't rush love; let it happen of its own accord"—I have heeded the second: "Should for some reason beyond your control the relationship be severed, wish the other well, and do not harbor jealous thoughts, for after all you have shared something wonderful together."

Whenever I think of Fred Wilkinson, which is often, I wish him well. If I could, I would will my love to him and trust that in some way, after I die, it will multiply in his life.

Maggie Hayes

My mother has a flair for personal correspondence. A friend of hers who had traveled from Kentucky to Richmond to attend Winnie's funeral told me, "Varina writes so engagingly, as if we see each other frequently. Indeed, after I've read a letter from her, I feel as though we've just had a good, long visit." In letters to me, however, Mother lets her hair down about whatever's foremost on her mind at that moment—someone has infuriated her, or she's elated over a bit of good fortune. Until the most recent tragedy, the main theme usually revolved around her other daughter—Winnie had provoked her and they were not on speaking terms; Winnie was seeing someone secretly and did not want her to know; Winnie was ailing, but would be better soon. The first communication I received about what turned out to be my sister's fatal illness was not optimistic, but neither did it sound a cry of alarm:

> Maggie, dear—A quick note to let you know Winnie has scarcely left her bed since she returned from the Atlanta convention afflicted with gastric upset. I believe she may have

caught some rare germ in Egypt, which lay dormant in her system for months, then flared up when she traveled to the Deep South during the most miserable time of the year. On the train coming back, she had a clear hallucination of her own funeral. . . . Looking on the bright side, the village doctor seems competent, and I approve of his medicinal choices. But oh, how I wish I had gone down to Georgia in her stead!

That last was not true. Mother has never liked traveling to those crowded post-Reconstruction gatherings. She, Winnie, my little boy, and I were slated to travel on the special tour for the twenty-fifth anniversary of Father's inauguration, but my child came down with scarlet fever soon after we arrived from Colorado. Mother used that excuse to stay at Beauvoir, with us. Had we been on the train as planned, the general from Georgia would have asked Mrs. Jefferson Davis to fill in for her husband when he was too weak to greet the crowd. Winnie and I might have had our names called out and waved dutifully to the crowd, but there would have been no anointing of one of us as a symbol of the Confederacy—like the battle flag, and Father.

After Father died, the South criticized his widow for moving herself and Winnie to New York, but Winnie was not blamed for that decision. Except for a flurry of outrage over her engagement to a Northerner with Abolitionist roots, the old guard's devotion to its "Daughter" has not wavered in the twelve years since they gave her the title. Now, in the aftermath of her passing, they seem determined to deify Winnie Davis.

An energetic, prideful organization formed a few years ago, the United Daughters of the Confederacy, has taken on the proj-

ect of procuring a monument for my sister's grave. My mother
put that bee in their bonnets, then sent the committee chairman a paperweight angel, which she described as being one of
Winnie's favorite possessions, for the sculptor to use as a model.
I asked her if the women knew that object was given to Winnie by
the man they got up in arms over her almost marrying. "I saw no
reason to include that information," she replied.

We have commissioned a life-sized bronze statue of Father for
his tomb. The finished piece will depict him in the attire he most
favored, a frock coat suit and cavalry boots, holding a slouched
hat in one hand. Mother believes this image will help dispel the
persistent rumor that the President of the Confederacy tried to
escape his captors by disguising himself as a woman.

My recollection of that incident in the woods outside Irwinville, Georgia, is conjoined to another that occurred a few days
later. As Father was being transferred from the ship *Clyde* onto
a small launch for the trip to Fortress Monroe, near Norfolk,
the Yankee soldiers made cruel sport of seven-year-old Jeff Jr.
for begging them to take him to prison too. Shortly thereafter,
Mother, Winnie, Aunt Margaret, Robert Brown, Jeffie, Willie,
and I were put off the *Clyde* when it docked at Savannah. Mother
had assumed that Father, as a defeated head of state, would be
taken to Washington, D.C. Instead, he was treated with utmost
contempt as a traitor who had led an "uprising."

I was aware of stares of curiosity, hostility, and pity as we
trudged under military guard to the Pulaski Hotel, carrying
what was left of the possessions we had brought with us from
Richmond. Most of those had been confiscated in the woods or
on the ship. Fortunately, Mother's sister Margaret had managed
to conceal a collection of Father's papers and books in her trunk,

which, after we arrived in Canada, would be placed in safekeep-
ing at the Bank of Montreal. We were insulted by Northerners
in the hotel's dining room and on the street. Mother seldom
left the hotel except for brief walks at night with Robert Brown.
Although we had no family friends to turn to in Savannah then,
there was an outpouring of gifts to us of direly needed clothing
from local residents.

Mother was not allowed to correspond with Father. After reading in the daily journals that her husband was in a dying condition, she wrote imploringly to Dr. John Craven, the physician at
Fortress Monroe, whose name she had found in a newspaper:
"Can these tales be even in part true? I have so often tended him
through months of nervous agony, without ever hearing a groan
or an expression of impatience. . . . Will you only write to me one
word to say that he can recover? . . . If you are only permitted to
say he is well, or he is better . . . The uncertainty is such agony."
After her first letters went unanswered, she wrote again, humbly
thanking the doctor for "ministering to his necessity" and assur-
ing him, "I daily give thanks to God that he has raised you up as
a present help in my husband's time of trouble." Eventually, the
prison director replaced Dr. Craven for having become too solici-
tous of the prisoner Jefferson Davis.

Mother spent much of that summer's confinement compos-
ing letters to people who wielded significant influence. She had
no qualms about asking the winning side to show charity and
compassion to the South's vanquished leader; he most certainly
would have extended mercy to them, had the situation been re-
versed. During the War, Father was known for being softhearted
and not punishing deserters from the Confederate army, unless

they joined the enemy camp. His wife proclaimed him innocent of any involvement in the vile murder of President Lincoln and vehemently refuted the rumor that the President of the Confederacy had tried to elude the enemy by disguising himself in women's clothing. She pleaded that he be treated humanely and that she be allowed to be with him during his incarceration. She would read the text aloud to Aunt Margaret and me—not for our approval or comments, but because the transition from written word to rhetoric added another dimension to her purpose and resolve. Then she would look for ways to get the missives past the inspectors.

The one that made the most impression on me was an eight-page letter to the husband of one of her close friends. It was hard for me to believe the courtly, amiable Montgomery Blair had a connection with Father's enemies. I did not know that Mr. Blair had been President Lincoln's Postmaster General, or what that title implied. In my mind, generals of the South had been brave men on horseback who consulted with my father then rode off to do his bidding on their battlefields. Seeing the address on the envelope, I closed my eyes and prayed that by some magical turnaround of time and events we would find ourselves in the nation's capital, where we used to be, and where all the power was. Mother would be happy again; Father would be famous in a good way instead of a bad way; and we would be invited on Sunday afternoons to Blair House, where the Blairs' daughter Maria and I would stare out a well-positioned window at the constant promenade on Pennsylvania Avenue.

During that summer in the Pulaski Hotel in Savannah, I would read and reread the copy my mother had kept of her letter to Mr.

Blair. Even now, thirty-three years later, I remember almost word for word her description of what to me was the most disturbing part—

> Just before day the enemy charged our camp yelling like demons. Mr. Davis received timely warning of their approach. He started down to the little stream hoping to meet his servant with his horse and arms. . . . Knowing he would be recognized, I begged him to let me throw over him a large waterproof wrap, which had often served him for a dressing gown, and which I hoped might so cover his person that in the gray of the morning he would not be recognized. As he strode off I threw over his head a little black shawl that was around my own shoulders, seeing that he could not find his hat. . . . When he had proceeded a few yards, the guards around our tents with a shocking oath called out to know who that was. I said it was my mother.

And I can hear the shimmer of desperation in Varina Howell Davis's clear-as-birdsong voice, just as I did on that deceptively bright May morning in 1865.

Yesterday, when I expressed concern that Winnie's elaborate monument might overshadow Father's, Mother said with exasperation, as though I'd bothered her unnecessarily, "I have made sure that will not happen. The figure on hers will be seated; his effigy will be standing."

But I have a feeling Winnie's angel will be larger-than-life, as she seems to be.

Mother was unusually pensive this morning. "Are you all right?" I asked.

She said, "I was thinking of Mary Chesnut. Of my deceased women friends, she is the one I miss the most. Do you remember, when the leaky train had stopped in Camden, South Carolina, that she and her husband came down to the cars to see us?"

"Yes," I said. "And they took us out to Mulberry, where we had a lovely, though meager meal. It seemed so safe there, I wished we could stay."

"No place in the South was safe then, but Mary was not a handwringer. She could find levity in most situations. Everyone knew the War was coming to an end, and one of the men at the Chesnuts' spoke as though the struggle was already in the past: 'The reason we fought was not to keep the system of slavery intact; it was to defend ourselves and our families and our property against an invading force that was hell-bent on destroying all of us and everything we owned. The anti-slavery fanatics had stirred up such hatred for the South, we never stood a chance.' Seeing how worked up the fellow was getting, Mary said calmly, 'And yet, the occupying Yankees are contemptuous of the people they have set free. As reported in Richmond, a too-grateful Negro barber threw his arms around a Northern general and hugged him in a close embrace. The Yankee freed himself and shot the man dead; he said it was time to stop that damned nonsense.'"

Mother pressed her hands to her eyes. "The anecdote was too cruel to be humorous, but I laughed."

I said, gently, "No, you didn't. If you had laughed even once during those terrible weeks, I would have remembered it."

Father's final illness began in early November 1889, when he set off alone on an excursion to Brierfield. He would not let Mother accompany him. I believe he realized the trip would be his last to the place where as a young man he had embarked on a different course, and he wanted to revisit that time, which had nothing to do with his wife. Or rather, not with this wife. Strangely, considering her jealous nature where he was concerned, Mother had made us respectfully aware of our father's great love for his first bride, Knox Taylor, for whom he left the army to become a Mississippi planter. His brother Joseph had provided the land, but Father cleared it and built much of the house himself.

Although Brierfield never became the happy homestead he'd envisioned, the place has had a colorful history. When the Union gunboats began to come upriver, Uncle Joe did the prudent thing and left the area. Both his plantation, Hurricane, and Brierfield were soon occupied by contraband slaves who had followed Ulysses S. Grant's troops during the invasion of Mississippi. The Union general's stated purpose was to make of this fertile property "a paradise for Negroes." Uncle Joe had seen to it that Father's library and other possessions were stored in the attic of a friend's house, but someone informed the soldiers of the location of the Rebel president's personal property, and the place was plundered. Carpets from Brierfield were cut up for souvenirs; the draperies were used for tents. Word reached Father that the Yankees had found a small portrait of him in one of the boxes; they made a game of stabbing the likeness, over and over, until the canvas was shredded. Like many Southern plantations, Hurricane was torched by the Yankees, but Brierfield was left standing. After the War, Uncle Joe sold the whole tract of Davis Bend to Ben Montgomery, the slave he had taught to read when they

were boys together, and who as manager of the plantation com-
missary had shared in the profits. Ben and his sons were to pay the
note off gradually, but crop failures due to worm infestation and
a severe flood that turned the peninsula into an island drove the
Montgomerys into greater debt. In 1881, the Mississippi Supreme
Court returned ownership of Davis Bend to Father and the other
heirs of Joseph Davis. Ben Montgomery's son Isaiah prospered by
establishing a successful all-black colony, composed mostly of former slaves of the Davis plantations, near Cleveland, Mississippi.
My mother communicates regularly with Isaiah, who was the only
black delegate to the 1890 Constitutional Convention.

The last time we were together, shortly before she embarked
for Egypt with the Pulitzers, Winnie said, as though practicing
on me what she might tell some stranger who was ignorant about
the old South, "Our mother and her brother-in-law Joseph Davis,
even though they couldn't stand each other, were of the same
mind about helping the Negroes advance. They were more far-
sighted on that subject than most of their peers, including our
father. Uncle Joe had provided incentives to his slaves to learn
how to be responsible for themselves and their families—"

"You know so much, you should hire yourself out as a governess," I said.

"I may come to that."

"No, you won't. Eventually, you will fulfill Mother's dream and
marry one of those wealthy, portly suitors she finds for you."

Winnie shuddered. "That projection makes me feel as if a cat
is walking over my grave."

"I've never heard you use that expression before."

"I learned it from a friend in Paris whose mother was a practi-
tioner of Voodoo. They were from New Orleans. . . ."

At that moment, Mother came into the room, and Winnie's face, which had become animated with whatever she was about to tell me, assumed its habitual enigmatic expression. I should have shown more interest in whatever secrets she had an impulse to divulge. I have never been particularly curious about how it must have been for her, as a perpetual debutante who allowed herself to be feted and courted but shied away from commitment. The thought of being passed from one dancing partner to another, year after year, is repugnant to me. Although Mother has hinted that Winnie had other proposals of marriage besides Fred Wilkinson's, Winnie never gave me that impression. She did not discuss, in any depth, either before or after their breakup, her feelings about Fred with me. From photographs, I could see why she would be attracted to him. He appeared to resemble, to a slight extent, our brother Jeff, and also the young Burton Harrison, with whom I had been secretly in love when I was a child and he was ever present at the Richmond White House, doing Father's bidding and being at Mother's beck and call. . . . Did Winnie have any love affairs during the last eight years of her life? If so, I hope the men were discreet. Living as far as I do from New York, Washington, D.C., and the gossipy cities of the South, I have not been exposed to any scandalous tales about my sister. If I had shown concern and interest, she might have felt free to confide things to me that she wouldn't tell our mother, and I would not have judged her. At least I think I would not have. I have just closed my eyes and said aloud, in case her spirit is hovering around, "Forgive me, Win. I should have done better by you."

For the first leg of his last journey to Brierfield, Father boarded a New Orleans–bound train that conveniently stopped at Beauvoir for him. He had booked passage on the steamboat *Leathers* from New Orleans to Vicksburg. That stint of travel on the mighty Mississippi would have been the high point of his trip. He covered the last few miles to Davis Bend in an open cart and a bone-chilling rain, awoke the next morning at Brierfield with deep-chest bronchitis, and stayed in bed for three days. After his wife received a mysterious message from him that began, "Nothing is as it should be," and a telegraph of concern from the plantation manager, she set out for Brierfield. As she departed New Orleans on the *Laura Lee*, a riverboat of the same line as the *Leathers*, Father was reboarding the latter at Vicksburg. The boats met below Natchez and she was transferred to the other vessel.

"How did she know he was on board?" Winnie asked, when she returned from Europe and wanted an account of every single thing I knew about those weeks before and after Father's death.

"It's a dramatic story, either way. She had been praying she would get to him quickly, when the revelation came to her that he had left Brierfield and was on his way to New Orleans. As soon as she spotted the *Leathers*, she knew he must be on it and insisted the captain of the *Laura Lee* let her board that one. The other version is that Captain Leathers's son, who was piloting the ship that had Mother as a passenger, learned that her husband was on the other one. He brought his ship alongside, and when Father awoke the next morning, there, watching anxiously beside his berth, was his wife."

"What if the boats had collided during that exchange?"

"You can put that question to her. She's all yours now. As a welcome-home present, I've decided to give you my entire share of Mrs. V. Jefferson-Davis."

Winnie looked as if I'd slapped her.

"I'm sorry," I said. "That was a mean-spirited joke."

"It probably did you good."

It well may have. After that exchange, I had a period of reprieve from a recurrent memory I never shared with Winnie. In the final days of the War, on the train that took us from Richmond, my mother would chant softly in rhythm with the rotation of the wheels, "God, please save us. Don't let them murder my children."

If my strong, brave mother was terror-stricken, how could I not be? But at least, I had reasoned, the baby would be spared that worry: Those frantic prayers would go right over Winnie's head.

The reunited Davises were met at the dock in New Orleans by Dr. Chaille and Jacob Payne and transported by ambulance to the Paynes' house at the corner of First and Church Streets, in the Garden District. The residence was then occupied by the Paynes' daughter and son-in-law, the Charles Fenners. Father was installed in a downstairs bedroom, where his wife could monitor visits from relatives and friends. He apologized to Mrs. Fenner for being trouble for her and told Dr. Chaille, "It may be strange to you that a man of my age should desire to live, but I do. . . . However, if it is God's will, I must submit, and I am not afraid to die." The physicians put him on a regimen of quinine and cordials, and Mother continued to administer the expectorant and calomel she had begun dosing him with as soon as she saw him. She was still trying to give him medicine when he spoke for the last time: "Pray excuse me, I cannot take it." The last words to flow from his pen had been written in the autograph book of Alice Trainor, the young daughter of the manager at Brierfield: "May all your paths be peaceful and pleasant, charged with the best fruit, the doing good to others." After a month-long decline that was peaceful, graceful, and filled with dignity, my father died in the first hour of Friday morning, the sixth of December 1889.

He had forbidden Mother to inform me or Winnie, who was abroad with the Pulitzers, of his illness, but I had read about it in a newspaper and was on my way to join them. I got as far as Fort Worth, then missed the connection that might have put me in New Orleans in time to see him before he died. The first thing I heard when I arrived in the city was the death knell of hundreds of church bells. Later, there would be the sound of muffled drums, which Mother said reminded her of the War that had taken so much out of her husband.

"The War took a lot out of you too," I said.

The remark seemed to surprise her. "Yes, I suppose it did."

His body had been transferred near midnight from the private residence to a council chamber at city hall. As I arrived there, the glass cover of the coffin was being removed for the sculptor to make the death mask. The Confederate president had been laid out in a gray suit. The *pater patriae*, whispered by nuns as they knelt briefly at the catafalque, would be reiterated in speeches and articles over the next week. He would have been surprised to hear himself referred to as father of a country that had taken away his citizenship. Journalists in both North and South, including some who usually were hostile to the man, would decry the fact that in Washington, D.C., where Jefferson Davis had served as Chairman of the War Department, flags were not lowered on any government building. During the five days he lay in state at the city hall in New Orleans—beneath Union and Confederate banners and a wreath of electrified bulbs that gave off a future-worldly glow—thousands had filed by the casket. Although a published account would note that the body was "remarkably well preserved," there were signs of decomposition by the time the coffin was placed on a black-draped caisson for the three-hour procession to Metairie Cemetery, where his wife had given consent for his temporary interment in the Army of Northern Virginia tomb.

Virginia, Mississippi, Alabama, Georgia, and Kentucky vied for the honor of providing the final resting place for the Confederate president. He had expressed a wish to be buried beneath a live oak tree at Beauvoir but had left the decision of where his remains would lie to his wife. Beauvoir was ruled out immediately; that was the last place she would wish to be buried when her time came, and the land was too low-lying. In July 1891, my mother wrote to the "Veterans and Public of the Southern States" an eloquent explanation of her decision to accept the offer made by Fitzhugh Lee, for the State of Virginia: "The most strenuous efforts of his life had been made upon her soil and in defense of Richmond, as the capital of the Confederate States. . . . Every hillside about Richmond would tell of the valorous resistance which he initiated and directed with tireless vigilance."

The transfer took place in late May 1893. The coffin was taken from Metairie Cemetery to Confederate Memorial Hall in New Orleans for a formal lying-in state; then Winnie and I accompanied it to Richmond on a special train that traveled slowly and made frequent stops. The South turned out full force all along the route. The diminutive station at Beauvoir was hung with wreaths; friends and former neighbors came aboard there to visit with us in the family car. In spite of the rain, elaborate ceremonies went on as planned in Montgomery; thousands paid their respects at the bier in the Alabama Capitol, where Father had taken the helm of the incipient Southern Confederation. At the station in Danville, Virginia, they sang the hymn "Nearer, My God, to Thee."

Mother joined us in Richmond. Jubal Early, wearing Confederate gray (like my father, he seldom appeared in any other color), escorted her in the procession to Hollywood Cemetery. It was a splendid day. In the late-spring sunshine, polished muskets and swords glittered like stars. The caisson that transported Father's remains to Metairie Cemetery had been drawn by six black horses. This time, the horses were white. Among the gold lace and tall plumes were tattered ensigns of various origin and style—the simplistic Bonnie Blue banner with a single white star, which cropped up in the first months of Secession; the Stars and Bars flag, which was not easily distinguishable in the thick of fighting from the Union's Stars and Stripes; and the square St. Andrew's Cross emblem of the Northern Army of Virginia, which became the official Confederate battle flag.

My sister and I did not indulge in much conversation with each other during that train journey. Her demeanor was that of a tragedienne playing her most dramatic role, yet I knew it was not an act; she was truly suffering. Winnie was closer to Father than I ever was. He had spent more time with the boys than with me, which was to be expected; when Winnie was born, the joy of a new baby in the house helped offset his grief over the death of his son Joe and the responsibility he had to face every day of that last dreadful year of the War. I have heard Mother say that, during the time they lived in Fortress Monroe with Father, Winnie had unlimited access to his affection.

He was an innately kind and sensitive man, but I don't believe he realized that revival of father-daughter closeness, which he instigated at a time when Winnie was almost a young woman, might be damaging to her.

According to journalists, Winnie was the first American woman to be honored with a full military funeral. (The person for whom she was named intends for that honor to be accorded to her also; while the details of Winnie's were still fresh in her mind, Mother composed a set of instructions for her own entombment and has given copies to both Addison and me. On mine, she wrote: "When I die, don't you go around in black. It is bad for your health, and will depress your husband.") The procession began at the Narragansett Pier station. Winnie's coffin was escorted by an honor guard of Union Army veterans on a special train from Rhode Island to Richmond, where the watch was turned over to a contingent of Confederate Army veterans. From the pageantry involved and the attendant publicity, you might have thought that Winnie Davis was the American equivalent of Joan of Arc.

When she was four, Winnie said she wished I could be a real mother to her.

"Why?" I asked.

"So I would have one to spare."

"I'm not old enough to be anybody's mother," I said.

"But what will happen to me, if ours dies?"

"In that event, I would take care of you. I do most of the time anyway."

"Do you promise?"

"Cross my heart and hope to die," I said.

"Good, then. That's a big load off my mind," Winnie said, in unconscious parody of the woman we had just been speaking of.

My sister was the neediest person I have ever known—but not for worldly goods, as might be expected, since the company she moved in exposed her to luxury far beyond her means. What she thirsted for was an ever-flowing font of affection. When she was six or seven, Win would ask other children who had been summoned to play with her, "Do you love me?" If one said "No," she would punch the child with her fists.

When I became engaged to be married, Winnie begged me not to leave her. I didn't leave her—although, as it happened, by the time she returned from Germany, I had moved with my husband to Colorado. Had we remained in Memphis, she could have visited us often, and Addison would have been a good influence on her. Neither of our parents seemed inclined to discipline Winnie. I recall one occasion when Mother took us with her to a large social gathering of some kind. Winnie was not yet walking alone, but she was trying to; I kept a firm grip on her pudgy hand and watched to be sure no one stepped on her. Apparently we did not make as grand an entrance as Mother would have wished, as she clapped her hands to get attention, then exclaimed effusively, "I want everyone to meet my baby. Winnie loves being with people."

As though she understood those words and took them as a command, Win yanked her hand from mine and held her arms up beseechingly to a stranger. Over the next hour, she was passed from one embrace to another, as though she were a tray of cakes. They nuzzled her chubby neck and tickled her under her dress; sometimes all I could see of her was that head full of springy curls bobbing as she was raised and lowered, kissed and squeezed. I silently willed my little sister to howl in protest at the next leering face that bent close to hers, but Win absorbed the adoration as though it were her due; when I finally rescued her, she had gone limp with pleasure.

It never occurred to me to try to dissuade them from enrolling Winnie in a school in Germany. They had left me in schools in Paris, London, Montreal, and Baltimore, and I rather enjoyed the changes of scenery and faces. But except for the two years Father was in prison, I was never away from either of my parents for more than a few months at a time. I missed my mother terribly during those bleak winters in Canada. Robert Brown and I held the household together; poor old Grandmother was not mentally stable, and Aunt Margaret moped about pining for the times when she was popular among the young sets in prewar Natchez and Confederate Richmond.

By the time Win returned to this country, the spoiled, demanding child had become a calm, seemingly self-assured girl, whose height and bearing made her appear older than her seventeen years. Despite the highly publicized article she later wrote condemning the fashionable practice of sending American girls abroad for their educations, that long sojourn apart from our strong-willed parents was the making of my sister, just as my moving with my good husband beyond easy reach of those parents has been the making of me.

After we learned of Winnie's illness, Addison wired my mother that I would come immediately to be of assistance however I might be needed. The response was swift and precise: "Not now. Maggie can visit when Winnie is well enough to enjoy her company." Weeks went by, yet I was not summoned. Shortly before noon on September 18, I had a nudge that Winnie was trying to tell me something. When Kate Pulitzer's telegram arrived informing us of my sister's demise, I had just placed my packed luggage in the front hall. Addison, the children, and Robert Brown, who had been with my father when he died in New Orleans, would come the following day. It was Robert who reminded me, after I shared with him the letter that mentioned Winnie's dream of her own funeral, that Jeff Jr. had a similar vision before he succumbed to yellow fever in the epidemic of 1878.

The deaths of my brothers (except for Samuel's, which occurred before I was born) are etched in my memory, but none so vividly as Jeffie's. Memphis was under quarantine due to an outbreak of malaria. No one could leave or enter the city, so our parents could not be with him during his last days or attend his funeral. Some months before, when Jeff Jr. had to leave Virginia Military Institute because of poor grades, my husband had found him a position at the same bank where he was employed. But for that bit of providence, my debonair brother would not have been almost engaged to be married in Memphis; he would have returned to Beauvoir and likely to a previous love, in Biloxi. Mother has never verbally blamed me for his death, but I believe she does so in her heart. Although I scarcely left Jeffie's side for all the days of his illness, I was preoccupied with the recent loss of our firstborn infant; I did not comprehend how seriously ill my patient was. Jeff Jr.'s dying, which was as sudden as if a bullet had pierced his heart, was a terrible surprise. I had assumed that God, having just taken my child, would spare my brother.

It's been almost six months since Winnie's passing, and my mother's eyes are still engorged with that grief. I had intended to spend the journey by train from Colorado Springs to Narragansett Pier giving vent to my personal feelings of loss—Win was my only sister, last remaining sibling—but when I reached my destination, the handkerchief I had clutched the whole way had not blotted a single tear. As I gathered up the basket of needlework I had brought to impress my mother and a stack of magazines Winnie would have enjoyed (I had been saving them to bring when she felt like seeing me), a wave of remorse engulfed me in a single despairing thought: I did not help her with our mother as much as I should have.

Unlike Winnie, I have never been inclined to give in to despair; I fight it the only way I know how, which is to substitute thoughts or memories that have strong optimistic potential. In this instance, I reminded myself of the time, a whole month of June, when Addison and I had Mother and Winnie as our guests in a leased cottage at Narragansett Pier. Win was like a kite cut loose from its string. It was pleasant, seeing her enjoy having whole days to herself and knowing that we were the cause of it. In the mornings, she would bathe in the surf, then relax in a seaside chair and read a book. Some days, she would set up her easel by the pier or the seawall and paint. Despite Mother's pleas that she not expose herself to the sun's damaging onslaught, her face and arms took on a lovely shade of biscuit tan that summer, and her hair lightened to the color of hay. Straw-boatered heads would turn to watch the tall young woman from Mississippi stroll the boardwalk and the water's edge as though her mind were a thousand miles away. In the afternoons, she would ride bicycles or go boating with other youthful vacationers she had found on her own, and most evenings, she would be called for by one of the men in this casual group. None of them showed any interest in getting to know her family. Winnie never seemed concerned about the credentials of her male companions, although Mother would caution her to be selective and not waste her time or risk her reputation by being seen in unacceptable company.

With Winnie thus occupied, it fell to me to keep Mother entertained during that holiday. When I complained to Addison, he reminded me gently, "But we agreed your sister should have every opportunity to spend time away from her."

Varina, Sr., either loves a place or can't stand it. During that visit, she became enamored of that particular spot of Eastern seashore, and in her canny, resourceful way, she set about making favorable impressions on innkeepers and others among the established community. Soon my mother and her companion-daughter had become regulars of the summer vacation colony at Narragansett Pier. I was surprised they could afford that annual holiday, but I didn't ask the question—not even of Addison, who, if he wasn't actually providing the wherewithal, likely knew the source of it.

When I arrived at the terminal on this sad mission, several people were there to greet me. The head of the delegation explained, "My dear Mrs. Hayes, your mother is too devastated to leave her rooms, but she is eager to see you. This morning she told me, 'Margaret will be my mainstay during these dark days.'"

Margaret? I could not remember a time, other than when she ordered invitations for my wedding, when my mother has ever referred to me by my real name.

Riding with these well-meaning strangers to the hotel, I felt disgruntlement give way to practical resolve. There would be much to do, and a large part would fall on me. Mother had gone completely to pieces at both of Father's funerals. At least Winnie was around to help me with her during the second one. The pretty little maid Margaret Connelly, whom I had met on previous visits in New York, answered the door with such a weepy face I wondered if my mother had expired too. The foyer and parlor were crammed with stiff floral arrangements and standing sprays, some in the shapes of hearts and crosses. But the scents of flowers do not mask the smells of illness and death. My eyes had begun to water and itch as soon as I set foot in that suite, and bile was rising in my throat. As I unpinned my hat, the servant who shares my name and doesn't have to answer to a glib alteration of it said softly, "Mrs. Hayes, Mrs. Davis said for me to tell you her nerves are completely frazzled, she's had no relief from the pallid opiates the doctor provided—her own medications have been forbidden her by that man—and she's in her bedroom, waiting for you."

What was I supposed to do? Impulsively, I followed the first inclination and gave my mother free access to all the vials and bottles that the efficient Margaret, obeying the doctor's instructions, had put beyond her reach. Mother was like a zombie on the train to Richmond and during the funeral, but on the return trip, she began to shake off the lethargic effects of her own potions; by the time we got back to the Rockingham Hotel, she had come to her senses.

The next item on the agenda was to get her moved from the hotel at Narragansett Pier back into the cluttered, four-room apartment in New York. When I unlocked that door, she waded into the stuffiness and eased herself onto the cushioned ledge of a bay window. "I love this view of the park," she sighed. "Winnie liked to take solitary walks there. I would sit here and watch her stroll along a curving path until she disappeared into the trees; then I would try not to be anxious until I saw her re-emerge. In the winter, wrapped in beaver, with her hands inside the exquisite ermine muff the Austrian count had given her, she looked like a European princess. She once said Central Park in the snow reminded her of Karlsruhe, and I asked her if that was a good memory. She replied, 'No, but it was eerily beautiful. That is where I learned that beauty can be terrifying.'"

My mother put her face close to the dirt-streaked glass, as though that effort might produce the vision she longed for. After a moment, she said glumly, "We should not have left her at that school as long as we did. Shortly before he died, your father said to me, with great sadness in his voice, 'We have done our youngest a grave disservice. We severed her so completely from her roots, there was no chance of any real re-attachment.' That Winnie appeared to have a foreigner's perception of this country especially distressed him. After her return to us, she read his treatise, then informed him the States' Rights philosophy he had championed was unrealistic for a nation as 'unwieldy' as this one. She would try to change his thinking about various aspects of the conflict, as though rehashing a chess game. He was both amused at her audacity and hurt by her expressing a viewpoint that wasn't altogether compatible with his."

"Winnie was too intellectual and analytical for her own good," I said. "The people who idolized her, those masses she talked down to from the podiums of the Lost Cause, did not know her at all."

Mother waved that comment away as if it were a housefly. "She earned every drop of their devotion. Winnie continued that role long after she tired of it, because she thought your father would have wished her to do so."

"And also, because she had become dependent on the acclaim. She had no intention of relinquishing her celebrity." I heard my voice go shrill with pettiness, but plunged on: "While Winnie was making charming speeches on those makeshift stages, I was making a home for my husband and children. In case you don't remember, some of that duty can be quite grueling."

My mother had both hands firmly pressed on her chest, as though to calm a wildly beating heart. I never know if such gestures are calculated to create an effect, or whether she believes she is about to go into catatonic shock. After a moment of catching her breath, she said softly, "My darling Maggie, you have heeded the most honorable calling a woman can have. If our line continues, it will be through you and your precious offspring. You are the exemplary daughter every mother dreams of having."

I did not look at her. My eyes were brimming with tears, and I was afraid I might glimpse a trace of mockery in hers.

After my mother finally came back from Europe, still maintaining she would never join her husband in another woman's house, she made a prolonged visit to Addison and me in Memphis. She complained to others that I asked her to leave, but the truth is, my husband was able to convince her that accepting Mrs. Dorsey's invitation would put a better face on an awkward situation. The transference was anything but gracious on Mother's part. Immediately after our arrival at Beauvoir, she created a terrible scene over nothing and ran screaming into the woods. It took a lot of cajoling to calm her. I believe she had suddenly realized, in what she would call a flash of divine intuition, that her rival was not a woman but the seductiveness of that house and setting; it was obvious that her husband had settled in and would never want to move again. After Mrs. Dorsey died and Father became the owner of the property, his wife found her own niche there. Varina Howell Davis's energy and homemaking talents would render Beauvoir even more beguiling, and for the next nine years, a steady stream of visitors—friends, our numerous relatives, and strangers—would be treated to Southern hospitality that may have been somewhat Spartan on occasion, due to the Davises' lack of provender, but was never provincial.

Mother had a cupboard built of cypress to hold her Staffordshire china and the everyday blue-and-white willowware. She supervised construction of a pair of octagonal, upholstered benches, which provided seating in the wide, central hall. When tourists came from other states and Europe, she would point out items of special significance: the quilt made for the president by "hundreds" of Confederate women; the French console and pier mirror from the home of Napoleon I, which she had purchased on a trip to Paris; a cup and saucer that had belonged to Lord Byron; and a picture album that had been stolen by a Union soldier and returned to them from Independence, Iowa, by the soldier's father. She would caress the marble head of her firstborn, Samuel—the small bust had been rescued during the pillaging of Richmond—and run her hands lightly over Winnie's oil painting of the Davis coat of arms.

According to Mother, Winnie's beau Fred Wilkinson, on his first visit, reacted to life at Beauvoir as though it were totally different from any place he had ever known. He had been surprised to see photographs of Abraham Lincoln and the martyred Abolitionist John Brown in the collection Father had put together of famous men he admired.

Oscar Wilde, a famous man Father did not admire, had named Jefferson Davis as the person he would most like to see on his American lecture tour. At Mother's invitation, Mr. Wilde visited

Beauvoir between his appearances in Mobile and New Orleans. That evening, as frequently happened, Father was not feeling up to prolonged entertainment and retired to his room after dinner. Mother and Winnie were enthralled by the brilliant conversation they shared with the visitor who, after they too retired, walked alone for hours on the moonlit beach in front of the house. Mr. Wilde left a portrait of himself inscribed, "To Jefferson Davis in all loyal admiration from Oscar Wilde, May '82."

Winnie made a will shortly before she left for Egypt last year. I was not surprised to learn she had left Beauvoir to our mother; they were of one mind in wanting the property to become a memorial to Father and a home for indigent Confederate veterans. A few weeks after my sister's funeral, Mother insisted that she and I make a pilgrimage to Beauvoir, to decide what should be left there and what should go to the Museum of the Confederacy in Richmond and other repositories in New Orleans and Montgomery. We have just finished this prioritizing. She wept to see what was familiar but had been long out of sight and mind, such as the dressing gown and slippers her husband had favored but would never wear to the table—even when he was feeling poorly—out of respect for her.

Although Mother and Winnie had brought some of Father's things with them when they moved to New York, there was still much to be disposed of: papers and documents, cigar cases, pipes, tobacco pouches, and curiosities of the War, such as the hollow doll in which morphine and quinine had been smuggled and a bar of soap that had conveyed a secret message from England for Judah P. Benjamin. She picked up each item, as if holding it in her hands could impart something more of him. Then she did the same with my sister's odds and ends—the driving whip and guitar, a red satin-lined work box and a messy paint box, and the dainty little watch purportedly given to Winnie by Princess Charlotte (but Winnie never seemed to recall the occasion).

Although I had never lived in that grand old house, seeing my parents' bedrooms again made me nostalgic. Father's, with his large, plain furniture, opened onto the porch and an expansive vista of the sea. The leather trunk at the foot of his bed had been with him to the Mexican War and Europe. Mother's room, which adjoined his and had a view of the rose garden, was more inviting, with canary yellow walls, an overstuffed chair, her airy bentwood rocker, the sewing machine she had acquired in Washington (and had enthusiastically endorsed in the manufacturer's advertisement), and the tall tester bed with its sky-colored canopy. A homemade fan of wild turkey feathers lay on a table, probably exactly as she'd left it when she and Winnie went to live in New York.

Watching her caress the canopy of the crib in which each of her children had slept, I felt closer to my mother than I had in years. That same day, without her knowledge, I wrote to her friend Mrs. Carrie Phelan Beale and requested the name "Jefferson Davis–Varina Davis Memorial Library" be used at Montgomery's First White House of the Confederacy, which would also be the recipient of many of the family's artifacts. I explained, finally, "She is now too old and feeble to do for others as she has always done. I know Winnie would agree with me in wishing our mother's name honored where she was beloved."

Now we are back in the apartment that overlooks Central Park, and I am provoked with her again. Every time she tells me how terrible it is to outlive one's children, I must bite my tongue not to remind her that I, too, had my firstborn taken from me and that the younger three Davises were almost as much my children as hers. I helped take care of those real-life babies when I might have been playing dolls, because our mother was otherwise involved. However, I grant her this: The pursuits that occupied her during those years were not frivolous. She would bustle about the plantation in her calico dresses with a ring of keys jangling at her waist. She cut out and sewed garments in the same serviceable fabric for servants at Brierfield, whom she never referred to as slaves. She nursed and dosed them when they were ill and saw to it that any who wished to had the opportunity to learn to read and do sums. There, and later at Beauvoir, Mother did much of the cooking, preserving, and gardening herself. In Washington, she dressed stylishly and was impeccably groomed. As someone wrote back then, "Varina Howell Davis is like a fruit tree in bloom; she has blossomed in the nation's capital."

She was sorely disappointed when Mississippi seceded from the Union and her husband resigned his Senate seat, because it meant they would leave Washington immediately—yet she had confidently expected to return to the nation's capital in the not-too-distant future. Jefferson Davis had held his own with all the political factions. A highly regarded statesman, he had not been in favor of Secession; he could speak to the sentiments of the pro-Unionists in Boston as well as to those of rabid dis-Unionists in Charleston. With his wife's encouragement, he had begun gathering his speeches into a pamphlet for distribution. Although my father never admitted that he wanted to run for President of the United States, others were convinced the timing was right, and that the stage was set for him to become a viable candidate. And my mother had not given up that dream. I was present when she told the clever Negro seamstress Elizabeth Keckley, who made her fine gowns for the Washington scene as well as more practical attire for life on the plantation, "We'll be back here when my husband becomes President of the United States." Later, when that quotation appeared in a book written by Mrs. Keckley, Mrs. Jefferson Davis denied having said any such thing.

In Montgomery and Richmond, she helped her husband forge a government and advised him on everything from the state of his health to cabinet appointments. I was proud that my busy, energetic mother considered me capable of taking on adult responsibility when I was seven, eight, and nine years old, and with her as my lodestar, I believe to this day that I did whatever she required of me to the best of my ability.

Another fragment has popped up unbidden: In Memphis, as I waited to walk Winnie home from school, she came out with a triumphant smile lighting her face. "Maggie, I know the real name of the War now. It's the War Between the States."

I had to burst her balloon. "That's not its only name. It's also known as the Civil War, the War of Northern Aggression, Mr. Lincoln's War, the Yankee Invasion, the War for Southern Freedom, the War of the Rebellion—now that's one you must never, ever dare to call it around Father or Mother—and the Recent Unpleasantness."

"Oh. Well, then, which should I call it?"

"The last."

That night at dinner Winnie said to Father, "Aren't you glad the Recent Unpleasantness is over and done with?"

He glanced at Mother. "I didn't know it was. But yes, indeed, I'm heartily glad to hear it."

Winnie's forthcoming coronation as queen of the most extravagant of all Mardi Gras balls was supposed to be a carefully guarded secret. Of course, Mother passed it on to me weeks ahead of time, so that I could start moving heaven and earth to get my husband and myself to New Orleans. I read the letter silently, then said to Addison, "Whatever can she be thinking of?"

He waited with slightly raised eyebrows for me to provide the answer.

"It's embarrassing for me to explain, even to you," I sighed.

"Well, please try."

"You will recall that Winnie made her bow to society in New Orleans. During that festive coming out in the 1883 Mardi Gras season, she was presented in the courts of masked balls and reigned as queen of one of them, the Knights of Momus. Now, nine years later, she is slated to be queen for another of these organizations, the Krewe of Comus. Mother has reminded me—although I never knew it to begin with—that Father had a special admiration for this men's secret society because it started right back up the year after the War ended."

"So what do you find embarrassing?"

"The fact that she has interfered with plans that were made months or years ago. The daughter of a prominent family in New Orleans had already been selected to wear the Comus crown in the coming season. In Mother's words"—I found the place, and read verbatim—"'This young lady graciously relinquished the honor on learning that Winnie was to be in the Ladies' Court, because she could not, in good conscience, put herself ahead of the Southern President's daughter.'"

"That was a noble gesture," Addison said.

"The girl probably had no say in the matter. A committee or ball captain was coerced into replacing her with Winnie. Mother will stop at nothing when she wants to accomplish a goal. This time, it's as though she suddenly decided that you and I should return to Memphis and have another church wedding, to attract attention to the family. 'The Davises are still here! Don't forget us!'"

"Perhaps your mother really is convinced that Winnie will benefit from another round of revelry in the city that puts a lot of stock in that sort of thing. And Winnie must agree with her, if she's going along with it."

"I doubt my sister was informed before the decision was made. If Winnie balked because of the obvious age difference between her and the other, younger women being presented, Mother would say that doesn't matter in the least, because she will be the prettiest, the most poised, et cetera. I suspect Winnie just gave in on this one because the deed was a fait accompli when Mother informed her, and living with that woman would be near impossible otherwise."

Addison said cheerfully, "I suppose we must make the best of the situation and be supportive."

"I don't go to the veterans' conventions to support Winnie's performance in that arena, and I have no intention of traveling to New Orleans to see another variation of the same. But what excuse can I use?"

"We have a prior commitment?"

"Mother would expect us to cancel it. Perhaps we should plan to be there, and then at the last minute, one of us can come down with something."

Addison offered, "I could get the measles. I've never had those before."

The invitation, which unfolded into an exquisite depiction of a lotus blossom and arrived in an envelope with a gilt crown embossed on the flap, was so splendid I almost changed my mind. Mother had informed me (in strict confidence; I was not to reveal a single detail) that the pageantry, including the parade, was designed by a foremost artist in that medium as a series of tableaux around the theme of "Nippon, the Land of the Rising Sun." The queen's elaborate costume of Japanese silk with a jeweled sunburst collar and belt had been made in Paris according to the measurements of the previous nominee and had to be let out in the seams and made longer for Winnie. The jewelry she would wear, also the tiara and scepter, came from France. Mother had been given a peep at the splendid gold cup that would be Winnie's coronation gift.

Later, after they had returned to New York, I sent them a sincere letter of regret that we had been unable to attend the festivities, especially the parade of floats and the ball at the French Opera House. I knew I should have followed Addison's advice and been supportive of my sister and mother in this undertaking, if only by swelling the number of family members in attendance. Winnie never mentioned the subject to me, but Mother wrote a full, glowing report: "As the Queen was led down from the dais to promenade around the floor, the applause was deafening, and I have never heard so many compliments paid to anyone as Winnie received that evening. Among her attentive escorts were two distinguished, quite eligible gentlemen—one a widower who lives in New Orleans; the other a near-nobleman from London—so, let us hope something develops along either of those lines." If something ever did, I never heard of it. Later, Mother would write, rather resignedly, "The portrait of Winnie in the exotic, Oriental costume is quite mysterious looking, and more than one person has noted its resemblance to Da Vinci's painting of the Mona Lisa. The analogy is appropriate. Even for me—perhaps, especially for me—Winnie is not an easy book to read."

Addison has been like a real son to my parents. We had not been married a full year before he had to come to Father's rescue in a financial matter, and unfortunately, that became a pattern. Hardly a month goes by that Mother doesn't write to my husband requesting assistance. She thanks him promptly, profusely, and piteously: "Whatever would this family have done without you. . . . "

But she doesn't express anything more than perfunctory gratitude to me for stroking her forehead, rubbing her feet, recording and acknowledging numerous tributes in memory of Father and Winnie, spending these weeks with her when I am needed at home, and for the promise she extracted from me this very morning, with my hand on the Bible: that I will not die before she does.

Alfred Wilkinson

OCTOBER 17, 1906

I have just read of the death of Mrs. Jefferson Davis. Spotting the prominently featured obituary provided a moment of elation, as though I had won a long-waged competition—but there was no competition, and no winner.

The last time I saw Mrs. Davis was at Winnie's funeral in Richmond, Virginia, and then from a considerable distance. Hoping to be inconspicuous, I had sat on a back pew during the service in St. Paul's Church and stood well apart from the graveside gathering. I would have liked to speak to Winnie's sister, Mrs. Addison Hayes, whom Winnie had referred to often and lovingly as Maggie, but that lady stayed close to her mother, the person I wished most to avoid. Over the next days, I debated with myself about writing a note of condolence to Mrs. Hayes and finally decided not to; since I had not really known her, and considering the way my relationship with the family ended, the communication might seem to her inappropriate. It occurred to me later that, had I approached Maggie Hayes or observed her at closer range that day, I likely would have noted mannerisms that reminded me of Winnie. In photographs, they did not resemble each other;

the older daughter seemed to me to favor their mother, and Winnie their father. When I received an engraved acknowledgment for the floral wreath I had sent, I thought perhaps the envelope had been addressed by Winnie's sister, as the handwriting did not appear to be that of their mother. Although I have long since destroyed Mrs. Davis's letters—which toward the end of our association became quite infuriating, even insulting—I would still recognize that bold, arrogant script.

Those I recognized in the large gathering either pretended not to see me or nodded in my direction and quickly averted their attention, except for Kate Pulitzer, who, after the crowd began to disperse, came straight to me and pressed her cheek to mine. "Dearest Fred," she murmured. "I am sure our darling girl knows you are here." I did not admit it then, but I concurred with that conjecture; at one particular moment during the burial service, I had such a strong sense of Winnie's presence I wanted to search for her.

Kate had sent the message informing me of Winnie's death before it became general knowledge. Reading her gently worded revelation, I had experienced a sense of release, which did not last, of course. I will never be cut loose from Winnie. But over the years, I have managed to rise above my hatred for the contentious person who drove the wedge between us.

As is her custom, Marion, the eldest of my three sisters who live with me, arose early and perused the morning paper before putting it neatly refolded at my place. She waited until I had served myself from the sideboard before asking, "Do you plan to attend this funeral too?"

I knew what she meant by that "too."

"No," I replied.

Josephine and Catherine, having already murmured "Good morning, Brother," in tandem according to their birth rank, gazed at their congealing porridge, waiting for me to say grace over it.

"Good." Marion would have said more, had I not silenced her with a glance and proceeded with the blessing.

I have been back to Hollywood Cemetery only once since Winnie's rites, and that was to see her monument, which had been erected by an organization of Southern women who call themselves the Daughters of the Confederacy. Presumably, they appropriated the title from the singular version, which was conferred on Winnie when she first began traveling with her father to those Lost Cause circuses. Thus laureled, she became famous not only in the formerly Confederate states but throughout the country and abroad. My mother said, when I returned from Mississippi and informed her that the engagement had been broken, "Perhaps it's for the best. You would not have liked living in that garish sort of limelight. It borders on the notorious for a young lady to be referred to familiarly by her first name—and a nickname, at that—by masses of people she doesn't know personally. How could Mrs. Davis have allowed her daughter to assume such a public role?" After a moment's further reflection, she added, with horror, "Oh, Alfred, do you suppose your connection with that family has made our good name notorious?"

"No, I think we managed to do that on our own," I said. Mother placed her hands over her ears and shook her head, imploring me not to elaborate.

When I learned, from an article in the *New York World*, that a small figurine of an angel that purportedly had belonged to Winnie had been submitted as a model for the monument, I wondered, from the description, whether it was one I had given Winnie as a memento of her first visit to Syracuse. The impressive marble sculpture in the Richmond cemetery did not bear much resemblance to my recollection of the alabaster trifle I had purchased, but I liked the idea that Winnie might have kept it.

The date of my only pilgrimage to the Davis family plot in Hollywood Cemetery was close to what would have been the thirteenth anniversary of when we were introduced. That occasion I recall as though it were last week. The first thing that struck me about Winnie Davis was the color of her gown, which brought to my mind the small golden-orange flowers that had flourished in my grandmother's garden. The next was the fact that a substantial amount of Miss Davis's tawny skin was visible. I had thought Southern girls dressed chastely, with lace covering their shoulders and upper arms, yet Winnie's arms and shoulders were tantalizingly bare. Later, after she had returned to Mississippi and I had identified the flower from an illustration in a botanical encyclopedia, I wrote to her: "At the Emorys' reception, as we were being introduced, your lovely image brought to my mind a delicate blossom, which I have since learned, through scientific research, is called a nasturtium. But should you prefer, I shall be happy to change the comparison to a rose or a lily. . . ."

She responded, "Your having likened me to a flower you had to look up the name of is more imaginative, therefore more of a compliment, than the usual analogy of comparing a girl to roses or lilies. Although that particular blossom is not in my mother's garden, she has described it to me: 'The nasturtium comes in the colors of the sun and the moon and tends to hide beneath its foliage.' As mothers are wont to do, mine asked why I had asked the question, and I replied, 'Just curious.' Of course, I could not tell her about our special friendship, since we have agreed to keep that secret for the time being. . . ."

Below her scrawled signature (for all her erudition and impressive vocabulary, Winnie's penmanship was like that of a young boy) was a postscript: "The idea of having foliage to hide beneath is appealing to one who places a high value on solitude and privacy. You should know that I tend to have a very nast(urtium)y disposition at times and should be left alone, as I am not always good company."

I was too smitten then to take that warning seriously. It was only after all was said and done, and could not be unsaid and undone, that I began to understand the situation in simple terms. I could hold my coat over Winnie's head in a rainstorm, but I could not shield her from the black cloud that seemed to overtake her suddenly and without warning. Nor, it seemed, could I protect her from the insidious manipulation of the woman who had brought her into the world.

Yet the parent I had been most apprehensive about was her father. In the two years after we met, Winnie had made several trips to my state, during which she had become acquainted with my friends and family, before she gave me permission to visit her milieu in Mississippi. And then I had to insist on it, for propriety's sake. Since her mother allowed Winnie to grant my urgent request, I assumed the Davises had received a good report about me from our mutual friends, the Emorys.

I was on the train, headed South, when Winnie informed her mother that I was more than a casual friend. When Winnie repeated the conversation to me, I could visualize her saying the words quickly, with her chin thrust out: "Fred and I are in love, and he intends to ask Father's permission to marry me."

She quoted her mother's reply: "If you'd told me ahead of time how important your visitor is, I would have made Charlotte Russe for his welcoming dinner. As it is, we're having a rather mundane blackberry cobbler."

Although Mrs. Davis and I would become adversaries, I must credit her with having had an open mind about me in the beginning. As she herself would assure me, my sweetheart's mother was "immediately and most favorably impressed" with my appearance, manners, and background: Six years out of Harvard (and six years Winnie's senior), I was established in the practice of law in a city where my family had been prominent since its founding. According to Winnie, the morning before I was to arrive that afternoon, her mother had tried to pave the way by softening Mr. Davis toward the idea of his daughter's being courted by a Northerner. She told the former president I shared his political views (I was then and still am a Democrat, and my father had been a delegate to the party's national convention in 1876). She also informed him that I was quite scholarly and had the greatest admiration for *The Rise and Fall of the Confederate Government.* That part was not true. I had found Mr. Davis's opus such excruciatingly hard going that I gave up after the first hundred pages. When I explained to Winnie that these volumes, which she so graciously had sent to me, were intellectually beyond my grasp, she laughed. "Oh, Fred, nothing is beyond your grasp. It's just not your cup of tea. I understand, and so would my father. But don't bare your soul to my mother on the subject."

Winnie said her father had nodded noncommittally when his wife informed him a friend of Tom Emory's in Syracuse, New York, was coming to visit Winnie. When she mentioned the prospect of my eventually becoming a son-in-law, his response was, "Never. Death would be preferable." Winnie first reported to me that he uttered only the word "Never." A few minutes later, she corrected that version, because, "Even at the risk of hurting your feelings, I do not want to keep the truth from you." If Winnie had realized truth can be veiled, and doesn't have to be put on display, I might have fought harder for her. As it was, her candor sometimes overwhelmed me and made me doubt that we could ever live happily together. But that prospect did not dampen my determination to marry her. And for five years, I never wavered in my hope of having that chance.

When I arrived at Beauvoir on that August day, she was fetchingly attired in a riding habit the color of dark leaves and waiting in the wood-framed gazebo that served as a minuscule station. I was relieved to see she was alone and hadn't come on horseback with a mount for me. Aware that Winnie was an enthusiastic and accomplished equestrienne, I had not yet admitted to her that I preferred for horses to be attached to vehicles. She was amazingly athletic for one of the fairer sex, but there was nothing unfeminine about her; Winnie was graceful in all her movements. I would watch her raise her arms to adjust her hair or a hat and marvel at how well synchronized that fluid motion appeared. As I emerged from the car, I knew my face was flushed with the expectation of seeing her again and finding her even lovelier in person than the ethereal vision I had carried in my mind for the two months since we were last together. When I leaned forward to place a kiss on her cheek, she put her arms around me and pressed her lips lingeringly on mine, as though oblivious of the train, which had not yet resumed its journey, and the likelihood that we were being observed from its windows. As we strolled along a densely wooded path to the house, she said, "You can, of course, expect a warm welcome—my parents are very hospitable, especially my mother, and they like to show off Beauvoir to visitors—but you must not bring up the subject of marriage."

Feeling rather cheated—I had memorized and rehearsed my speech before a pier mirror, as though I were about to argue in court—I said petulantly, "As one gentleman to another, I feel it is incumbent upon me to inform your father, at our initial meeting, that my intentions toward his daughter are entirely honorable."

"He knows that. He just doesn't want to have the conversation yet."

"Can you tell me what his primary objection might be to my suit?"

"The geography. You live in enemy territory."

"But you've said your parents have many friends in the North, such as the Emorys, who brought us together, and that those connections that were lost because of the War have been renewed in recent years, with no bitter feelings."

"It's not easy to explain. Darling, please be patient."

I treasure the fact that she used an intimate expression of endearment before I did. She was always a step ahead of me in showing affection. As we walked along that woodland path and conversed and got used to each other again, we paused occasionally to embrace, and as though heeding her own advice to me,

Winnie was careful not to let her hair or clothes reflect any disarray. I wondered how she could go so quickly from being impetuously foolhardy to being cool and collected. I did not know then that she had plans for us to return to that dark patch of forest on the following day and that there, on a cloistered spot beside a frantic brook, beneath the tallest pine trees I had ever seen, we would give ourselves wholly to each other in what would be the most sublime experience of my life. Later, we made love in other places, but the first occasion is the one I find most accessible to revisiting. Visualizing, in my mind, the hazy conjoined image of the two of us on that magical afternoon makes me feel as though Winnie and I are still and forever linked together.

Seated at the other end of the table, in the place that for a sadly brief time was our mother's, Marion pretends she is the hostess of my house. She watches me with a fond, sardonic smile, as though we are a married couple and she knows what I'm thinking. I suspect she dares to pretend, to herself, that I am the husband who never materialized for her. She has always had presence and was attractive in her youth, but the bank problems and the fire put a damper on her chances. If Marion didn't irritate me so, I could feel more compassion and admiration for this sister, who is two years younger than I, and who holds me in such high esteem. The other two, who were noisy, exuberant young girls, seem to have lost that vitality when they lost hope of being chosen for matrimony. It's almost as though they've taken vows of silence. Now, having dabbed at their mouths with large damask napkins—being careful to avoid the embroidered monogram near one hemstitched corner (my first gift to Mother after the fire was to replace the table linens that had been in her trousseau)—they wait for me to leave the table first. I established that routine last year, after Mother went to reside at the excellent care-giving facility Briarcliff-on-the-Hudson. As I leave the dining room without throwing a crumb of language to any of this trio, Marion's voice lifts like a bird on the wing: "Brother, will you be here for dinner?"

I disdain to answer (which she will rationalize as being due to preoccupation, not rudeness) and continue to the foyer, where I retrieve, from the hall tree, my hat and a gold-knobbed cane that belonged to my father. Walter has placed my leather case on a table next to the heavy, paneled door he is waiting to open for me. After I am delivered to my offices by the cab he procures, I shall concentrate on my work as a patent attorney, which I enjoy because I can lose myself in it for hours at a time, and also, it's quite lucrative. For the past twelve years, since my father died, my goal has been to restore what should have been my (or rather, our) inheritance. I am thankful I was able to provide my mother with some semblance of her accustomed manner of existence before she lost the ability to discern between what is gracious living and what is not. Those years in a modest house on a side street in Syracuse were hard on her; she became a recluse, under the pretense of being an invalid. But she liked living in New York, where she could take carriage rides without worrying whether or not people were staring at her. Had it not been for the stroke, I believe she would have regained her once formidable spirit and determination.

As it turns out, the meeting I had prepared for has been cancelled, nothing urgent awaits my attention, and I find myself gazing out the window at familiar surroundings I do not feel a part of, although in the three years since I moved to this metropolis, my clientele has more than doubled. It was a wrenching decision to pull up stakes in Syracuse, where my ancestor John Wilkinson opened the first law office. Since I could not in good conscience leave my mother and sisters behind—my father's will had named me as guardian of his minor children, who at the time he died also included Henry, my only brother—I brought them with me, and established our household in the West Fifties.

My mother did not protest the move. It wasn't as though we were leaving the house where she had spent the best years of her life. That one, which the newspapers at the time of its destruction referred to as a mansion, had gone up in flames on a midsummer night with a full moon; the cause of the conflagration was never discerned. We were all on the second floor in our bedrooms when a neighbor banged on the door, alerting us to the danger. Then that good man hurried up and down the street, rousing others to come to our aid. Henry and I had herded Mother and our sisters down the stairs and onto the lawn and had rushed back inside to retrieve what we could, when we heard a moan. I found George Jemison, our loyal retainer (Walter is his nephew), collapsed in the dining room. We brought the poor man out, but he could not be revived and subsequently died. The bucket brigade would not allow us to enter that furnace again. They did their heroic best, but only a few chairs and small tables were saved. The Persian carpets, portraits and other paintings, some exquisite bronzes, and virtually all the family heirlooms of jewelry, crystal, silver, and china, were consumed by the flames. Not a tree in the apple orchard behind the house was spared. It was as though that graceful hill I had sledded as a boy had suddenly turned into an avaricious altar, and our fine old house, which had graced the property with such dignity, was the sacrifice it demanded. But to what purpose? For weeks afterward, whenever she was not sedated by opium, my mother would cry out a single word: "Why?" At least my father did not live to see this tragedy.

Because of Father's death, which occurred a few months before I met Winnie, I almost did not attend the reception the Emorys had for her. I had sent my regrets, but on the day before the event I happened to see Tom, and he urged me to reconsider. "You've been the model son and heir. Now you deserve some reprieve from that house of mourning. Please stop in for awhile, Fred. I especially want you to meet Miss Varina Anne Davis of Mississippi. I'm sure you'll find her delightful company, and I understand she's unattached."

I had recently taken the black wreath off our front door, although my mother wanted it to remain for a full year. I was still grieving for my father, but I was ready to resume some social activity. I thanked Tom for the opportunity to reverse my previous response and assured him I looked forward to making the acquaintance of a young lady from the Deep South who was not someone's wife or spoken for.

That exchange reminded me of a former classmate's discourse during a drinking session in Cambridge shortly before we were to graduate. Chauncey Talbotton had just learned that his longtime sweetheart, whom he had counted on becoming engaged to as soon as he got back to Georgia, had eloped with another man. He said morosely, "Here's some advice, Fred, in case you ever need it. Girls of the South, especially those from the deeper states, can convince you they're sweet and tender as June corn. But they also possess a devilish streak, which comes from the fact that their daddies or granddaddies or both fought and maybe died in the War, and their mamas and grandmamas, having learned how to be tough because they had to, passed that knowledge on to them.

So be wary of any princess you meet from Alabama, Mississippi, Louisiana, or Georgia. She'll make you think you're the one—then, should she take a notion to, she'll break your damn heart without a backward glance."

Coming as it did, after what would prove to be a fateful encounter with Dr. Thomas Emory, I might have taken that recollection as a warning. On the contrary, I felt buoyantly optimistic at the prospect of meeting Miss Varina Anne Davis.

Mr. Jefferson Davis was strikingly distinguished looking, in a dapper, courtly, old-gentleman sort of way. He had a full head of silver hair and an immaculately trimmed beard. His posture was faultless, whether he was receiving guests or taking his ease in one of the oak rocking chairs, which according to his wife, he had constructed himself, along with other rustic odds and ends of furniture, when they first came to Beauvoir. (Mrs. Davis made it sound as if they had arrived there at the same time, but I learned from Winnie that was not the case.)

On my initial visit to Beauvoir, Winnie informed me, as soon as we had a moment in private, that her father obviously liked me, since he had invited me to accompany him that evening to the bath house, to watch the flounders. "He doesn't share that favorite pastime with many people," she said. I liked him immediately, although I found the close resemblance of Mr. Davis and his daughter disconcerting. The topography of sadness that mapped his face was a gossamer veil on hers.

The man was less austere than I expected. He seemed reserved, yet convivial enough; physically strong, but not robust. Within an hour of making his acquaintance, I watched him wade into a fierce fight between two large dogs, pull their snarling mouths apart with his bare hands, and emerge unscathed. When Winnie introduced me to her parents on their spacious front gallery, which was quaintly referred to as the porch, Mrs. Davis recited my biographical data as though the information would be new to me, as well as to her husband. He nodded in my direction after each point during that litany and smiled at the end of it, as though to say, "Good. Now we're through with that." Although she made no mention of my maternal grandfather, who had been actively involved in the American Anti-Slavery Society and a leading advocate for women's rights, Mrs. Davis noted I was "well-born and connected to New England's most illustrious families, including the Quincys and the Hancocks."

I was disappointed that Winnie's father would not entertain any discussion of my intentions and somewhat discomfited by the coquettish attitude of her mother. That Winnie and I were allowed to wander about the estate without chaperonage gave me hope that, in due course, we would obtain her father's blessing. I was surprised, to say the least, when the girl I loved (she was twenty-two then) seduced me on the second day of my visit. A small circle of blood on the back of her skirt indicated she had been a virgin. Winnie assured me that she would wash that spot from the garment and no one else would see it. I was greatly relieved to hear that her mother (who, I had already surmised, was acutely observant) would not be at the house when we returned and that her father would be in his library cottage. I felt very protective of Winnie and was glad I had maintained enough presence of mind to practice coitus interruptus. Assuming the display of ardor and her determination to become intimate were a result of her European education, I suggested with as much delicacy as I could muster that if we were going to indulge ourselves in that sort of pleasure, we should do so only at times when she would be least susceptible to conceiving a child. Winnie said, nonchalantly, "Of course, you are right to bring up that subject, but don't worry. A friend's mother has instructed me about timing and other methods of contraception."

I thought, with amazement, *Southern girls must really learn a lot at their mothers' knees.* "Other methods," I repeated. "Such as—?"

"There is a sheepskin sheath that, from the look of the thing, certainly appears to be trustworthy. I could order a supply for you from a source in New Orleans, and I can show you how to put it on—" She seemed as earnest as a tutor explaining a lesson to a backward pupil.

"That won't be necessary," I said. I might have laughed, had I not felt somewhat insulted that she should assume I was ignorant about the subject.

"Also, through the same source, I could procure a device called a cervical cap. And there's a very simple method that involves a syringe with an alum solution."

"Whatever you think best," I said, as though we were discussing the details of our wedding. In fact, I wished we were having that kind of conversation. Although she had been the instigator, I felt as though I had taken advantage of her. I have never been tempted to tell anyone about that aspect, or for that matter any other aspect, of my relationship with Winnie Davis. I have not allowed myself to show an interest in how she lived her life after me, and with whom she might have been keeping company. My friends have kindly avoided the subject; however, some years ago, a casual acquaintance told me he had attended Mardi Gras in New Orleans the week before and had recognized my former fiancée as the featured occupant on the most spectacular float in the parade.

"Did she look happy?" I asked.

"Her eyes were hidden behind a half-face mask, and I don't recall seeing her smile; I would say she looked resigned. During the ball, people were approaching the make-believe royalty to pay their respects. I'm sorry I didn't get in the line to greet Miss Davis. I would have conveyed your very best wishes to her—"

"If you knew me better, you would realize that kind of banter would have been very much out of line," I said.

"Well, I'm sorry I brought this obviously painful subject up. But now that I have, I'll add that the atmosphere down there, all that pompous chivalry, not just in New Orleans, but everywhere I've visited in the Old South—well, I can't imagine why they keep up the pretense."

The man had a point, but I didn't want to agree with him. I had been charmed by the South that Winnie inhabited.

Winnie's father and I never had the official talk, but on my second visit to Beauvoir, it seemed that he was taking my presence in his life for granted, and I dared to assume he had come around to the idea of having me for a son-in-law. His wife had all but guaranteed that would be the case. Yet later—after Mr. Davis had died, and after Mrs. Davis had formally announced our engagement and then informed the world of the postponement of the nuptials—I would be advised by a Major Morgan, the Davises' nearest neighbor on that rough-shell road in Mississippi, to give up my quest to marry Winnie. Morgan came to Syracuse and asked questions of my colleagues and friends before he presented himself at my office. As though I were a boy in need of mature guidance, the pompous old fellow addressed me as "son" and placed his hand on my shoulder: "Look at the situation from our standpoint. Your esteemed family has suffered a severe reversal of fortune"—he'd found out about the Wilkinson Bank's failure—"and you are not sufficiently established in your profession to support a wife and simultaneously provide for your mother and siblings, who should be your first priority." He then confided that supporters of the Lost Cause, of whom he was one of the most ardent, would like to see "Miss Winnie" establish what would be regarded as a royal bloodline for the South by marrying a grandson of one of the distinguished Confederate Generals Robert E. Lee, "Stonewall" Jackson, or Sidney Johnston. The last named, Major Morgan added gratuitously, had been Mr. Jefferson Davis's favorite of the lot. I heard the man out with appall and embarrassed anger. I knew he was someone Mrs. Davis leaned on for advice, and it was obvious she had dispatched him to do this dirty business. The colleague I was closest to, whom this Mississippian had approached quite openly, was aghast that I should be treated thus by the woman who had urged me, not so long before, to travel to Europe and provide emotional support to her grieving daughter.

Winnie was abroad with the Pulitzers when her father died. Her mother decided that she should remain with them in Italy and that I should come to visit her and try to cheer her up. When I arrived in Naples, Kate Pulitzer was waiting for me. Her husband, she explained, could not stand the noise in the harbor, so they had moved their group from the moored yacht to the Grand Hotel. On the way there, she assured me Winnie's current affliction of melancholic depression was easily explained. "She has been crushed by a massive feeling of guilt because she was not available to her father in his extremity. Winnie has said, many times these last few days, 'I would not have let him make that trip

to Davis Bend alone.' And, 'I should have been informed as soon
as he became ill; I could have got back in time to see him, and at
the very least, I would have been at his funeral.' Now that you're
here, I am sure her good humor will gradually return, and before
too long, she will be her delightful self again."

Kate's optimistic projection did not occur. Winnie stared at
me as though I were a stranger. When she spoke my name in a
dejected tone of voice, as though she were thinking, *Why in the
world is he here?* I wondered that myself. Instead of sending me into
a situation I was ill-equipped to handle, Mrs. Davis should have
crossed the Atlantic to minister, with maternal compassion, to her
suffering child. I could see Winnie's anguish was genuine, but her
personality had altered significantly since I'd last seen her; she
seemed suspicious of everything and everyone. The next day, during an episode of extreme delusion, she screamed at me: "If you
take me to an asylum, I will run away" and "My father will pistol-
whip anyone who tries to lock me up." She did not in my presence
show any outburst of temper around Kate or Joseph Pulitzer, so
one part of her must have realized that while she could rage at me
all she wished and I would not abandon her, she'd best not turn
on the people who were treating her to this sojourn.

Once Winnie got used to my being there with her, she required
frequent reassurance of my devotion. She even begged me to
make love to her. Of course, I could not take that liberty: Propriety did not permit me to lock the door when no one else was in
her room but the two of us, and at any moment, Kate or a servant
might rap on that door or, for all I knew, immediately open it, to
check on the patient.

Not that I wasn't attracted by Winnie's unusually wanton expression and the aphrodisiacal unkemptness of her loosened

clothing and tangled hair. She could not bear for the bedcovers to be over her—Joseph's physician (who supplied the laudanum and morphine that seemed to alleviate her misery for brief periods) explained that claustrophobia often sets in during periods of mental abnormality—and I lasciviously enjoyed these glimpses of her bare limbs and feet, especially when she was sleeping. It occurred to me that taking this wild-eyed creature of despair while she was unconscious would be just as thrilling as the rites she initiated in those deep, private woods at her family's estate.

As it happened, shortly before I was to return to the United States, my abstinent stance gave way. Winnie's vitality had revived sufficiently for her to be up and around. Kate said, to me, with the faintest tinge of a blush on her lovely face, "You and Winnie should have some time away from the rest of us. I've made arrangements for you to take her on a weekend adventure, the highlight of which will be a monorail ride up Mount Vesuvius on John Mason Cook's funicular. I have reserved accommodations at the charming inn at the base of the mountain. Mr. Cook has enlarged the restaurant, and I understand it's quite elegant."

I could not imagine any excursion that might be more problematical for someone with nervous problems than what I'd just heard described. I was also aware, as Kate apparently was not, that the volcano had erupted several times—most recently in 1872—and that its ashes had been distributed over all of southern Europe. Despite my misgivings about the venture, Winnie's face lit up when I told her of the plan. She said, "Kate is a dear. Some time ago, I mentioned to her that I had read a fascinating engineering study of the funicular railway and that I would love to take a ride on it someday. Are you familiar with the concept of single-rail construction?"

"Not specifically," I said warily.

"Fred, it is absolutely ingenuous. Longitudinally laid wooden stringers carry the one rail, upon which the central wheels ride. The funicular uses two cables, which are driven by a steam engine at the bottom and round pulleys at the top. Side rails, placed at an angle, are adapted to wheels that have axles projecting from the floors of the coaches, thus keeping the carriage upright—"

"All right," I said. "I'll take you on the ride, if you promise the carriage will remain upright. Actually, I would ride in it upside down if necessary, because I am so happy to see you looking forward to something again."

"What I'm really looking forward to are the nights at the inn," she whispered. "When we get there, you can tell the concierge we will not be needing that second room."

I was almost giddy with relief. I thought the darling girl I loved had returned.

And so she had, for awhile. That interlude, the last private time I ever had with Winnie, was as near perfect as anything could be. I believe she realized that our relationship was newly fragile, as a result of her unpredictable mood reversals of agitation and depression and my inability to pull her out of either, and that she resolved to keep herself on an even keel for those forty-eight hours. When I left the Pulitzer entourage in Florence a few days later, Winnie had begun to withdraw into another phase of grief, this one more inward. I hoped she would not scream at me when I bid her farewell. She didn't. In fact, she did not seem to notice I was leaving.

I had reported via letters to Mrs. Davis several times during the trip. I did not mince words; I thought she should know just how severely afflicted her daughter's state of mind was: "I know that Winnie has written to you. Perhaps you will see from her letters better than mine how difficult it has been for me to get her to discuss any commitment to the future. . . ." I suggested Mrs. Davis come over and get her. Winnie needed to be brought home one way or another. She could not travel alone, and it would not look right for her to travel with me, without a chaperone. I told Mrs. Davis that, in my opinion, it could take at least six months and maybe a year of tender care before Winnie would be ready to face the world again. I also advised the woman, "It would be cruel to broach the subject of marriage with her before next winter."

Nevertheless, soon after I returned in April, my engagement to Varina Anne Davis was formally announced by Mrs. Jefferson Davis. Northern newspapers made a great deal of the polarity: The daughter of Jefferson Davis, the only President of the Confederacy, was going to marry the grandson of the New England Unitarian minister Samuel May, who had traveled widely as an anti-slavery speaker and assisted in the rescue of escaped slaves from the South via the Underground Railroad. In the immediate aftermath of the announcement, defamatory letters were delivered to me, all with postmarks from the South. (One of the more galling accused me of being a "Negro-loving zealot" and warned that if I absconded with their "purest lily of the South" I would be hunted down and castrated.)

Two months later, in June, Winnie returned from Europe with the Pulitzers and was urged by various individuals and organizations to terminate the engagement her mother had announced.

In July, my family's residence, where nineteen years earlier my Abolitionist grandfather had died, was destroyed by fire. In August, Mrs. Davis posted another notice, stating that her daughter's wedding had been postponed until June 25, 1891, as Miss Davis did not wish to be married until at least a year after the date of her father's death. In October, I was summoned to Mississippi for a bitter confrontation with this woman whose emissary had caused me great embarrassment by coming to my territory to ask questions about my financial resources and look for scandal about my family.

"Admit it," Mrs. Davis spoke to me as though I were a common criminal. "You cannot afford to maintain my daughter in comfort and style, and you have not been honest about the appalling situation of your finances." Winnie was not present during the diatribe, but she came out afterward, and we had a brief farewell session. I do not recall a single word of what we said to each other, although I read somewhere that Mrs. Davis reported my last remark to Winnie was, "I shall never give you up." If I said any such thing, it was more likely, "I shall always love you." Even if she had been willing and strong enough to defy her mother then, I doubt I could have gone through with the marriage, knowing that woman would still be involved in our lives.

Much to my consternation, a few months later, Winnie and her mother moved to New York to earn their livelihood as writers. That development effectively ended my own plan to relocate there in order to expand my law practice.

Winnie had been dead for four years when I decided her mother could not do me any more damage and that the metropolis was big enough for both of us.

The only time I came near Winnie after that day was at a reception at the Pulitzers'; she looked as if she were seeing a ghost, and I suspect I did too. After she quickly changed direction, in order to avoid having to acknowledge me in that gathering, I took my leave. The next day, I sent Winnie a brief, sincere note, apologizing for any embarrassment or discomfort my presence at the party might had caused her, and in general, wishing her well. There was no reply, and I have preferred to believe her mother confiscated that missive and Winnie never saw it.

Recollecting fleeting glimpses of Winnie gives me weird pleasure. As she ascended the steps of a bus with a sweep of skirt caught up in a gloved hand, I recognized the strong curve of her calves and her slender ankles. In a crowded theatre lobby, I spotted her beneath a chandelier that seemed to focus all of its light on her auburn hair.

The first time Winnie visited my family at the James Street residence, she politely complimented her surroundings, but it was easy to see she had little interest in domestic decor, other than to take mental note of details to put into her novels. This seemingly callous indifference on her part irritated my mother. However, when Mother mentioned that her first cousin was the writer Louisa May Alcott, Winnie responded with enthusiasm. "There is no one in the world I would rather meet than Miss Alcott. When her novel *Little Women* came out, my sister received the book as a Christmas gift. She would read it aloud to me, a chapter at the time; then Maggie and I would pretend we belonged to the happy March family and lived in their cozy house." She turned to me and said with what appeared to be mock exasperation, but I knew was the real thing, "Fred, you have never told me you are related to a beloved, renowned writer of novels."

My mother, quite mollified, said, "Well, my dear, you certainly must meet Louisa. Fred, we should all take Winnie to Concord for a visit with our famous cousin."

Behind her back, Winnie mouthed: *Let's not take them.*

I explained to my mother that the two lady authors would have much to talk about; therefore, only Winnie and I would go to Concord, so as not to risk overtiring Louisa with too much company.

The journey from Syracuse to Concord took most of a day, but it was the best time of year in New England. Gazing out the window at the rich panorama of autumn, Winnie said, "How do you stand so much beauty at once and the knowledge that it will return again the next year?" That was an epiphany. I thought: *She has resolved not to let her parents and friends dissuade her from marrying me and living in my part of the country.*

Louisa awaited us at Orchard House, the family home she maintained with earnings from her popular children's books and the blood-and-thunder novels she wrote under a different name. Among the relatives who lived there were Lulu, the niece Louisa had adopted, whose deceased mother, Abigail May Alcott, had been an artist of some acclaim in Paris—Winnie was aware of Abigail's fame, also—and nephews who were the prototypes for the boys in *Little Men.* Winnie and my first cousin once removed greeted each other with ease and within minutes had convinced themselves and me that they were kindred spirits.

After making the introduction and participating in the polite exchange of pleasantries, I sat back to observe what I sensed would be inspired interaction between these gifted women, who

were a generation apart and had been exposed to vastly different perspectives. I doubt Louisa would have brought up the fact
that she had been a nurse at the Union Hospital at Georgetown,
D.C., but Winnie did and asked her questions about the experience. None of us had any idea then that within the next year
Louisa would succumb to effects of mercury poisoning she had
contracted during that wartime service. The thought occurs to
me now, as it has before: *Had Louisa May Alcott not died, Winnie
might have kept her commitment to marry me and live in Syracuse.* Being
within reasonable proximity of that calm wisdom, where Winnie
could count on finding encouragement for her own literary pursuits, would have helped offset the tedium of living so closely with
less interesting and more demanding female in-laws.

During that visit, as though she realized there would not be
another, Louisa allowed herself to be drawn out by Winnie's
brash curiosity. Was it true she had been tutored by the naturalist
Henry David Thoreau?

"I had lessons from him, but my education was chiefly in the
hands of my father."

Was her father the model for Mr. March?

"No," Louisa smiled in my direction. "I based the March girls'
father on my uncle, Samuel May, who was Fred's grandfather."

Winnie glanced at me with reproach. How could I have kept
this fascinating information from her? I knew how she felt; every
now and then, when she would casually refer to some remarkable
incident that had to do with her family in particular or the South
in general, I would wonder why she hadn't revealed that nugget to
me before. She and Louisa spent at least an hour discussing books,
particularly novels. Winnie described one that had been written by
a woman who had been reared in the North before coming South

with her husband, where she led a life of some hardship; Louisa remarked that the woman must have been quite resourceful to find the time and energy to give voice to her own inner muse.

"I can't imagine how she managed it all, especially with such a terrible husband," Winnie said. "I would want to get rid of a husband who tried to stifle me."

We were sitting, the three of us, beneath Louisa's arbor. I had been lulled by the cadence of their conversation and the pleasant surroundings. "What do you mean by 'get rid of'?" I asked.

Winnie turned to me as though she'd forgotten I was there. She said, "Women can easily do away with husbands. A dash of calomel in his morning coffee, day after day for several months, should accomplish the deed where no one would be the wiser." She wasn't smiling, nor was I.

Louisa came to our rescue. "Winnie is right; it would not be difficult, if the husband is trusting of the hand that prepares his meals. Who knows how many times a woman has got away with murder and felt no guilt because of the way she was mistreated, or imagined she was? But I believe most of our gender are inclined to be nurturing; therefore, they put up with those difficult husbands and, in fact, take just as good care of them as they would the worthwhile fellows. Some women don't realize how lucky they are, to get the latter variety, because they've had no experience with the other."

Winnie sprang up—she had been sitting on the ground, literally at Louisa's feet—and came to me and put her arm around my waist. Then, her face close to mine, she said, as solemnly as though repeating a vow, "I am quite aware of how lucky I am, to be spoken for by a man of the utmost worthwhile variety. Darling Fred, I promise to try not to be the death of you."

Louisa's eyes were shining with tears. She said it was a joy for her to witness such love between her favorite young man and his chosen young lady.

When I informed Winnie of Louisa's death, she wrote to my mother. The last sentences of that note of condolence puzzled the recipient and enlightened me more about the nature of my beloved: "I admired the beautiful, productive life your cousin Louisa had made for herself, with her art as its central focus. She had the loving security of being surrounded by family, without the complications and strictures of matrimony; and whenever she wished, she could retreat into solitude."

My secretary has brought in the morning mail, which included a package from a stranger. The contents are a notebook such as a grade school student might use, and this letter:

Dear Mr. Wilkinson, Sir:

For several years, I was employed as a maid by Mrs. Jefferson Davis. That service ended last fall, when I married. I felt badly about leaving her, but my husband-to-be did not require me to earn wages and wished me to become a housewife in my own right. I have heard, recently, that Mrs. Davis is severely afflicted with prostration of the heart. That sad news has made me aware that I must unburden myself of a responsibility I perhaps should never have taken on in the first place.

This notebook, which contains personal reflections of her late daughter, has been in my possession since September 18, 1898, which you may recall was Miss Winnie Davis's last day on earth. I helped care for her during what would be her final illness and was at her bedside when she passed away. Although

Mrs. Davis is practically a doctor herself when it comes to medicating, she did not spend a lot of time in the sick room with her daughter. I believe the lady must have known Winnie was not going to come out of this one, and she could not face the prospect of losing her.

During those last weeks of Winnie's life, I had seen her scribbling in this notebook or rereading what she'd written in it at an earlier time. Soon after she died, I retrieved the thing from beneath that hotel bed, where I had seen her put it. I'm ashamed to say, curiosity got the best of me, and I read it. Then I was in a quandary as to what to do with the notebook, as I knew Mrs. Davis might have a seizure on seeing some of what her daughter had written here, and also, I was aware that Winnie had not wanted her mother to know of its existence. I almost gave it to the other daughter when she came to stay with Mrs. Davis after Winnie died, but I thought better of that idea. If Mrs. Hayes decided to pass the book on to her mother, or even mentioned it to her, I would have some explaining to do. Next, I thought of their distant cousin who was Winnie's best friend, Mrs. Pulitzer. What stopped me there is, I am pretty sure that Winnie, although she was a writer by trade, would not want these musings to be published. But Mrs. Pulitzer's husband, since he owns a newspaper and Winnie and her mother had worked for him, might have a different opinion on that subject.

Mr. Wilkinson, whatever feelings you may harbor toward Miss Winnie Davis, I know you are a gentleman and that you will respect her privacy, and not share this journal with others. Winnie and I had only one significant discussion about you, which took place a few days before she passed away. My recollections of that exchange and the last day of her life are recorded in several loose pages from my own diary, which will be folded into the same envelope with this letter.

When Mrs. Pulitzer's maid pointed you out to me standing off by yourself at Winnie's funeral, I saw on your face the same steadfast, grieving love I'd seen just a few days before on hers, when Winnie was speaking about you to me. I resolved then to send you her last writings, but I never could get up my nerve. Now that Mrs. Davis is not long for this world, it seems an appropriate time.

> With every good wish,
> and I pray I am doing the right thing,
> Margaret Connelly Black (Mrs. Alton Black)

Occasionally, I have the midday meal in my office. Earlier, before my secretary brought the mail to me, I had asked her to place an order for me with a restaurant in the adjacent building. I shall wait until the repast has been delivered and consumed, and the tray has been cleared away, before I commence to read Winnie's journal.

By then it will be her favorite time of day. I am remembering one golden afternoon beside a brook at Beauvoir, in sultry, stalwart Mississippi, when she quoted to me a line from Tennyson's "The Lotos-Eaters": "In the afternoon they came unto a land, in which it seemed always afternoon."

Then, without taking her eyes from my face, she removed the pins from her hair and shook it free. As she began to unfasten the buttons of her primly high-necked blouse, I knew that this afternoon, and this girl, would be with me always.

Epilogue

Alfred Wilkinson died of heart problems on May 27, 1918, at Atlantic City, where he had gone to recuperate from a nervous breakdown. The Harvard Class of 1880's Fortieth Anniversary Report noted: "He will be remembered by his classmates in his college days as full of life, positive but good natured, companionable and with a sense of humor. He was a man of strong family affections. He never married."

Acknowledgments

For his astute advice and ongoing encouragement through all phases of this project, I am indebted to Richard Jordan. It was my good fortune to connect early on with Ruth Ann Coski at the Museum of the Confederacy in Richmond, who responded to numerous queries, steered me to other sources, and corrected errata. My deep appreciation goes to Director Nicole Mitchell, Courtney Denney, John McLeod, Stacey Sharer, and everyone else at the University of Georgia Press whose expertise and enthusiasm have contributed to the production of this book.

I thank Bill Muller for his interest and counsel; James Rogers, Jeanie Thompson, Isabel Sanders, Danny Gamble, and Robyn Litchfield for timely suggestions; Dodgie Shaffer, Mary Ann Neeley, and Anne King for tea and empathy (Anne's notes on Beauvoir and the Jefferson Davis Presidential Library were more helpful than my own); Tibby Elebash and her friend Avery Bassich for information about nineteenth-century New Orleans; Mary Lynne Levy and the book club for keeping me well read; and everyone who, in the last few years, has asked me if I'm writing another book.

I have taken a novelist's prerogative in allowing my imagination and intuition to embellish what is accepted as fact and legend about the Jefferson Davis family and their times. Dates have not been altered, with one exception: I moved the publication of Guy de Maupassant's first novel, *Une Vie*, from 1883 to 1881, so that Winnie could read it during her summer in Paris. In a few instances, text has been incorporated from the writings and correspondence of those on whom characters are based or who are referred to tangentially in the narrative. The sections labeled "Winnie's Notebook" are not based on actual journals or diaries; however, a fictional letter therein was inspired by an archived Wisconsin memoir by E. P. Arpin Jr., which was shared with me by his daughter, Helen Till, and brought to my attention by Tom Fitzpatrick.

The quotation that became this book's epigraph, which I didn't come across until the manuscript was almost finished, eloquently echoes a premise I began with: that Winnie Davis was a complex enigma, even to those closest to her. It didn't happen right away, but at some point during the early sessions of writing about her, I began to feel as though I had passed muster and been granted permission. When the serendipitous hunches (that novelists receive and have to decide whether or not to go with) increased in frequency, I even wondered if my protagonist might also be my collaborator.

Institutional repositories consulted include: the Harvard University Archives, Pusey Library, Cambridge, Massachusetts; the Ray M. Thompson Papers, McCain Library of the University of Southern Mississippi, Hattiesburg; the Robbins Papers and the Mary Stamps Papers at Wilson Library, University of North Carolina at Chapel Hill; Olin Library, Cornell University, Ithaca, New York; the Eleanor S. Brockenbrough Library, the Museum of the Confederacy, Richmond; the Jefferson Davis Papers, Rice University, Houston; the Rosanna Blake Confederate Collection, Marshall University, Huntingdon, West Virginia; Memorial Hall Confederate Museum, New Orleans; the Alabama Department of Archives and History, Montgomery; the Center for Southeast Louisiana Studies, Southeastern Louisiana University, Hammond; the Williams Research Center, the Historic New Orleans Collection; the Library of the Virginia Historical Association, Richmond; Nancy Burris, Librarian, *New Orleans Times-Picayune*; Records of the Third Regiment Georgia Volunteers of the Army of the Confederacy; the Southern Historical Association, University of Georgia, Athens; the Casemate Archives, Fort Monroe, Virginia; the Birmingham Public Library; the Montgomery Public Library; the Syracuse Public Library; the Onondaga County Historical Association, Syracuse; the New York State Historical Association, Cooperstown; the American Newspaper Repository, Rollinsford, New Hampshire; and the Sinclair Manuscripts, Lilly Library, Indiana University, Bloomington.

Selected Bibliography

Allen, Felicity. *Jefferson Davis, Unconquerable Heart.* Columbia: University of Missouri Press, 1999.

Anderson, E. M. Davis. "The Daughter of the Confederacy." *Montgomery Advertiser,* October 19, 1899.

Avary, Myrta Lockett. *Dixie after the War.* New York: Doubleday, Page, 1906.

Beidler, Philip D. "Caroline Lee Hentz's Long Journey." *Alabama Heritage* 75 (Winter 2005): 24–31.

Bleser, Carol K. "The Marriage of Varina Howell and Jefferson Davis: 'I gave the best and all my life to a girdled tree.'" *Journal of Southern History* 65, no. 1 (February 1999): 3–40.

Blount, Roy, Jr. *Robert E. Lee.* New York: Penguin, 2003.

Bradley, Chester D. "Dr. Craven and the Prison Life of Jefferson Davis." *Virginia Magazine of History and Biography,* January 1954, 50–94.

Chesnut, Mary Boykin. *A Diary from Dixie.* Ed. Ben Ames Williams. Boston: Houghton Mifflin, 1949.

Clark, Emily. "Racial and Religious Identity in Antebellum Natchez." In *Mississippi Women: Their Histories, Their Lives.* Ed. Martha H. Swain, Elizabeth Anne Payne, and Marjorie Julian Spruill, 4–20. Athens: University of Georgia Press, 2003.

Cook, Cita. "The Challenges of Daughterhood." In *Mississippi Women: Their Histories, Their Lives.* Ed. Martha H. Swain, Elizabeth Anne Payne, and Marjorie Julian Spruill, 21–38. Athens: University of Georgia Press, 2003.

———. "Women's Role in the Transformation of Winnie Davis into the Daughter of the Confederacy." In *Searching for Their Places, Women in the South across Four Centuries.* Ed. Thomas H. Apple Jr. and Angela Boswell, 144–60. Columbia: University of Missouri Press, 2003.

Cooper, William J., Jr. *Jefferson Davis, American.* New York: Alfred A. Knopf, 2000.

Coski, John. *The Confederate Battle Flag, America's Most Embattled Emblem.* Cambridge, Mass.: Belknap Press of Harvard University Press, 2005.

Davis, Varina Anne. *A Romance of Summer Seas.* New York: Harper and Brothers, 1898.

———. "Serpent Myths." *North American Review* 146 (1888): 161–71.

———. *The Veiled Doctor.* New York: Harper and Brothers, 1895.

Davis, William C. *Jefferson Davis: The Man and His Hour.* New York: HarperCollins, 1991.

Ferrell, Chiles Clifton. "The Daughter of the Confederacy—Her Life, Character, and Writings." *Publications of the Mississippi Historical Society* 2 (1899): 69–84.

Foster, Gaines. *Ghosts of the Confederacy.* New York: Oxford University Press, 1987.

Fraiser, Jim. *The Majesty of Eastern Mississippi and the Coast.* Greta, La.: Pelican, 2004.

Gehman, Mary. *The Free People of Color in New Orleans: An Introduction.* New Orleans, La.: Margaret Media, 1994.

Harmon, Rick. "They Were Soldiers." *Montgomery Advertiser,* October 31, 2002, Sec. D, 3.

Horwitz, Tony. *Confederates in the Attic: Dispatches from the Unfinished Civil War.* New York: Random House, 1998.

Jackson, Lily. "'Daughter of the Confederacy' and a Queen of Comus." *New Orleans Times-Picayune,* January 29, 1978.

Kane, Harnett T. *Bride of Fortune: A Novel Based on the Life of Mrs. Jefferson Davis.* Garden City, N.Y.: Doubleday, 1948.

LaCavera, Tommie Phillips, ed. *Varina Anne "Winnie" Davis, "The Daughter of the Confederacy."* Athens, Ga.: Southern Trace, 1994.

Landis, Dennis. "Samuel Joseph May." Unitarian Universalist Association. http://www.uua.org/uuhs/duub/articles/samueljmay.html.

Meigs, Cornelia. *Louisa M. Alcott and the American Family Story.* London: Bodley Head, 1970.

Monsees, Anita. "How the Daughter of the Confederacy Almost Became a Daughter of New York." *Heritage Magazine* 7, no. 3 (January/February 1991): 4–5.

Napier, Cameron Freeman. "A House Is Never Finished: The Anatomy of a Restoration." *Montgomery County Historical Society Herald* 5, no. 2 (April 1997): 1–5.

Rogers, William Warren, Jr. *Confederate Home Front: Montgomery during the Civil War.* Tuscaloosa: University of Alabama Press, 1999.

Ross, Ishbel. *The First Lady of the South: The Life of Mrs. Jefferson Davis.* New York: Harper and Brothers, 1958.

Sanders, Isabel, and Cindy Schoenberger. *The Historic Garden District: An Illustrated Guide and Walking Tour.* New Orleans, La.: Voulez-Vous, 1988.

Sinclair, Mary Craig. *Southern Belle: The Personal Story of a Crusader's Wife.* Phoenix, Ariz.: Sinclair Press, 1957.

Sullivan, Walter. *The War the Women Lived: Female Voices from the Confederate South.* Nashville, Tenn.: J. S. Sanders, 1995.

Swanberg, W. A. *Pulitzer.* New York: Charles Scribner's Sons, 1967.

Thompson, James West. *Beauvoir: A Walk through History.* Ed. Keith Hardison. Biloxi, Miss.: Beauvoir Press, 1988.

Twain, Mark. "The Black Forest and Its Treasures." In *A Tramp Abroad,* 137–45. New York: Penguin Classics, 1997.

"Uncovering the Real Lincoln." Special issue, *Time*, July 4, 2005.

Van der Heuvel, Gerry. *Crowns of Thorns and Glory: Mary Todd Lincoln and Varina Howell Davis, the Two First Ladies of the Civil War.* New York: Penguin, 1988.

"A War of Words about the Civil War." *Washington Post*, November 11, 2004.

Wilkinson, Israel. *Memoirs of the Wilkinson Family in America.* Jacksonville, Ill.: A. M., Davis and Penniman, 1869.